I would highly recommend this book. Just like the previous jaw-dropping tales it had me hooked from the start and intrigued by where it was going with its clever little twists and turns. At times, I would shake my head in awe at how the final outcome made me tut or laugh, albeit in a positive way. A true match for Roald Dahl's 'Tales of the Unexpected.'

A brilliant read.

Susan Crook – Late of Barton Bottoms

About the Author

I HAVE BEEN INTO CREATIVE WRITING FOR MORE YEARS THAN I CARE TO REMEMBER AND HAVE DABBLED IN MANY GENRES. HOWEVER, I HAVE ALWAYS BEEN FASCINATED BY 'TALES WITH A TWIST' AND IN THIS HUMBLE COLLECTION I WOULD LIKE TO THINK THAT I HAVE ACHIEVED SOME MEASURE OF SUCCESS. WOULD YOU AGREE? THE ONLY WAY TO FIND OUT IS TO READ ON

Derek J Rogerson.

25 more tales with as many twists as there was in my first volume of fantastic tales.

As before they all contain a common theme and unless your imaginative thought processes are as convoluted as mine, after each you will undoubtedly whisper under your breath,

'Well I never saw that coming.'

Dedicated to my family for their unflagging encouragement and to Sue my number one fan.

CONTENTS

A Ship By Any Other Name!

It was in the year of Our Lord 1861 that found John Briggs and Martha Jackson not just happy – but deliriously happy. From the port of Bristol, they had boarded the brigantine 'Amazon' on one of her early voyages as strangers and yet during the time that it had taken to cross the grey Atlantic, the pair had met, fallen deeply in love, had plighted their troth and had just been made man and wife by the ship's captain.

It was not surprising that they had been happy and contented in each other's company as they had boarded the ship with a common goal, to better themselves in the new world of America. John had worked, both as man and boy in the inn trade. His father had been a respected innkeeper before him so it was no surprise when his son had followed in his footsteps. Over the years, he had learned every aspect of running a successful hostelry from the brewing of good strong ale, the preparation of hearty food and how to deal with the rowdier of his clients when in their 'cups'. He had heard of the opportunities for enterprising young men in the Americas and so following the passing of his parents and with nothing else to keep him in England, and his pockets filled with gold sovereigns from his inheritance; he decided to seek his fortune in pastures new.

Now Mistress Fate is well known for having this peculiar knack of throwing like-minded people together and in this case her aim had been unerring. Martha had also spent her early years in many of the numerous inns and taverns in and around her home city of Bristol. She had started as a humble barmaid but thanks to her particular gift with figures, she had risen to the ranks of keeping the books in one of the more upmarket establishments in the city. It was unfortunate for her though that the landlord there was afflicted with the unsavoury malady of 'wandering hands', which had eventually resulted in him receiving a black eye and Martha out in the streets with nothing more than the clothes she stood up in. At least that's what the lecherous landlord had thought until he later discovered that a sum of £80 had somehow gone astray. It had been fortunate for Martha that this had been exactly the sum required to secure herself a berth on the good ship Amazon on its next voyage to New York.

The ship was barely out of the Bristol Channel when John and Martha had first spoken and within hours a bond had been forged between them that would ultimately result in their marriage. As the long days passed they talked of little else other than how they were to secure their fortune in the land of opportunity. Thanks to their dual experiences in the hospitality trade, it was therefore no surprise that they had decided to pursue this path......

It was grey and miserable day when they eventually docked in New York harbour and a sudden shower sent them scurrying to a tavern just outside the harbour gates. The interior of the little watering hole was dark and dismal, the ale sour and the food disgusting. It was little wonder that apart from a solitary drunk at the end of the bar, the place was empty. The conversation from the landlord fitted the surroundings perfectly and most customers would have been unhappy with his constant grumbling about the state of his business; but to John and Martha it was music to their ears.

"I'd sell up tomorrow if I could find a fool crazy enough to buy it," moaned mine host. It was a fact that in its current state, very few respectable customers would ever venture over the threshold never mind buy it but John and Martha immediately realized the potential in the run-down tavern. Its location was perfect for both landing and embarking passengers and between them John and Martha knew even then that they could turn this failed business into a thriving enterprise – and that is just what they did........

It was now 1872 and in just 11 short years the enterprising couple had turned a dingy waterfront tavern into one of the most thriving and popular hostelries in the whole of New York. Not only that, they had opened up another dozen or so similar establishments up and down the eastern seaboard and such was their good fortune that they now wined and dined with the cream of American society. However, they never quite lost the common touch and were often found helping in one or other of their hostelries.

In November of that year, John received a letter from one of their wine suppliers in Italy, inviting them to spend the festive season enjoying Italian hospitality. It had been some years since they had last enjoyed a holiday together and it was an easy decision to make in accepting the kind offer and John immediately started making the necessary travelling arrangements. He returned later that day and flushed with exhilaration he told Martha the wonderful news.

"Remember how we met on the good ship Amazon all those years ago," he said to an equally excited Martha. "Well would you believe that it's sailing to Italy on November 7th and should get us there in plenty of time for the Christmas celebrations? They don't usual carry passengers any more but I've had a word with the captain, who by coincidence has the same surname as me and made him an offer that he just couldn't refuse; so pack your bags my girl – we're off to Italy on the vessel where we first met. Oh! I forgot to mention, it's not called the Amazon now. The ship has new owners and is now called......." Before John had time to complete his words he was interrupted by an almighty bang from the road outside the building. Martha gasped and clutched desperately at John's arm. "Relax Honey," he said comfortingly, "Remember what day it is? November 5th. It's only some ex-brits letting of fireworks – and just think in two days we'll be on the high seas on our favourite ship – now what could be nicer than that?.....................

The voyage to date had not been the peaceful one they remembered on their first crossing. The 282-ton brigantine had battled through heavy seas for two weeks to reach the Azores. John had toughed it out as best he could but poor Martha had spent much of the time in their tiny cabin, plagued with terrible sea-sickness. It was in the early evening of the 25th, an evening that had turned out to be unnaturally calm and John and Martha were sharing the delightful interlude on the deck. The skies were clear and they spent some time identifying the different stars and constellations that filled the dark sky. "Look John look, I believe that is a shooting star and it appears as though it's going to pass right over us." John directed his gaze to where his wife was now pointing and agreed that it did indeed appear to be a shooting star. The peculiar thing was, as it approached it appeared to be slowing down, and even more peculiar as it passed over the ship it appeared to stop altogether.

"What in heaven's name can it be?" whispered Martha anxiously. "

"It appears to be some sort of craft that can fly," replied John looking closely now at the large circular silvery object that hovered over the ship at a height of about 50 metres. Around the rim were uniformly spaced bright lights that shone with a colour and luminosity never previously seen by human eyes? From deep within the craft issued a harmonic hum that was just in the range of human hearing. All the crew were now assembled on the deck gazing in awe at the sight above them. Without warning a ray of light flashed from the strange vessel enveloping the ship from bow to stern. All below were bathed in the strange light and in a heartbeat – they were gone..............!

All trace of life has departed from the now soundless ship. Not a purr from a contented cat in the galley is heard, or the scratching of a disturbed rat in the bilge, or the murmur of a concerned human voice on the deck disturbs the absolute silence of the scene. Through that long night the vessel drifted aimlessly on the still calm sea and as the dawn broke the early rays of the sun lit up the

ship's prow highlighting its name - Mary Celeste!

Meanwhile in a galaxy far beyond the Milky Way a small group of bemused people in 19th century attire opens their eyes as if from a long sleep to find themselves on a sandy beach that is bright blue, lapped by a sea that is a vivid red while a deep purple sun shines brightly from an emerald green sky.

Acid Jack

"I just need a little more time to pay you back Jack," pleaded the terrified young man; his frightened eyes darting from the badly scarred face of Acid Jack to the thuggish acolytes that attended him.

"Did I ask you for more time before I loaned you the two grand?" responded Jack, paraphrasing Ebenezer Scrooge's cruel reply to his destitute client so many years previous.

"Yeh, I r-read that book at school," stammered the cowering victim, hoping this tenuous connection would soften Jack's menacing tone,

"Well I aint gonna send you to the workhouse fella if that's what you're expecting; I got something a bit more up to date and touchy-feely for you. "said Jack with a contemptuous sneer. Before the poor wretch had time to consider this reply, Jack had reached into his trademark camel overcoat and retrieved a large glass phial containing a colourless liquid. Removing the stopper, he flung the contents at his victim and laughed aloud as the solution burned deep into the previously youthful and unscarred face, giving off the aroma of bitter almonds as it found its mark – It was prussic acid – Jack's 'persuader' of choice.

Jack, you see was a very successful and quite ruthless loan shark and very few had ever reneged on paying back a loan, even at the extortionate interest rates that he charged. This impressive success rate was no doubt due to his highly unusual but very persuasive incentive for ensuring timely payback, that of throwing acid into the faces of the laggards – Hence his street name of 'Acid Jack'.

One might ask as to why Jack Forshaw, his given name, had chosen this unusual method of control to encourage his 'clients' to meet their monetary obligations. It transpired that some ten years previous he had been forging a successful career for himself in the chemical industry. He was also engaged to young Helen who worked in the typing pool and was to be married the following spring. Everything in his life was going to plan and a more contented man would have been difficult to find anywhere in the country.

All this happiness unfortunately was destined to end abruptly on that fateful day when a large glass container had exploded just as Jack was passing the bench on which it had been placed. The highly corrosive contents of concentrated prussic acid had caught him squarely in the face and as well as now been scarred for life, the pain that had ensued had been truly horrendous – A pain so agonizing that even he could never wish on anybody – except perhaps if it was used as a not so friendly persuader.

This unfortunate incident had not only affected Jack physically but had also soured his previous happy-go-lucky temperament and had turned him into a vicious and unfeeling thug who now spread terror and fear through the mean streets where he plied his nefarious trade. Despite a generous compensation and severance package and a long period of convalescence, he had been unable to secure any form of lawful employment in the area, due in the main to his now quite hideous appearance and it appeared that no self-respecting business were inclined to hire a freak for fear of the mayhem that such an appointment might incite among both staff and customers.

His fiancé, though initially sympathetic to his facial disfigurement, quickly came to realize that no matter how hard she tried, she could not imagine spending the rest of her life with such a freak (plus the fact that the managing director's son had recently been casting a lustful eye in her direction).

On reflection, although somewhat disappointed to lose Helen's affection, Jack had been content that his career path had stalled as with the money from his settlement he was able to start up in the loan business, especially when he realized just how many desperate people there were out there anxious to make use of his services, despite the eye-watering interest rates that he demanded. However, there was always the few that were tardy with their repayments but it was surprising how quickly most of them came to their senses when faced with Jack's interpretation of the 'acid test'. Such was the effectiveness of this terrifying deterrent that very few had actually experienced it. The very thought of being on the wrong end of an acid shower was usually enough for them to settle their account.

Over the years, Jack's success in the business had been reflected in the magnificent ten-bedroom mansion that he now owned in the nearby commuter belt. It boasted all the trappings of a successful businessman including tennis courts, a croquet lawn and a superb Olympic sized swimming pool that was undoubtedly his pride and joy.

It was whilst returning from a particularly successful day in his state-of-the-art Lamborghini that his thoughts had wandered and he just didn't see the young lady in his path until it was too late to take evasive action. The poor woman had no chance of surviving the inevitable impact and was pronounced dead on the spot by the attending paramedics. A little of Jack's previous caring nature kicked in and when he learned that his 'victim' had been the wife of one of his former work colleagues from the chemical factory, He had attempted to redress the unfortunate situation by offering the poor guy a substantial sum of money as compensation for his reckless act. The inconsolable widower refused to accept this offer, calling it blood money that could never hope to replace the unconditional love of his erstwhile spouse and vowed to have his day in court and so Jack was subsequently arrested and charged with causing death by dangerous driving.

Jack may have been sorry for the demise of the unfortunate young woman who had inadvertently wandered into his path on that eventful night - but not that sorry. A guilty verdict would no doubt have seen him incarcerated for some considerable time and despite his initial altruistic feelings, Jack had no intentions of spending more time in a prison cell than was absolutely necessary. Fortunately, his ill-gotten gains allowed him to hire the services of probably one of the best criminal defence lawyers in the business, none other than Sir Archibald Fanshaw QC.

After the initial briefing, Sir Archibald informed him that there was no way he could escape entirely the due processes of the law but he was confident that he could get the initial charge of causing death by dangerous driving, which usually carried a substantial prison sentence, reduced to the lesser charge of driving without due care and attention, which gave him a reasonable chance of a much shorter sojourn as a reluctant guest of HM Prisons.

Sir Archibald had been as good as his word and after being able to 'procure' a witness to state on oath that the unfortunate victim had stepped into the road without looking and was also locked in earnest conversation on her mobile phone at the time. The judge had little choice but to reduce the charge and the sentence that followed was a joke. 28 days in the local jail and a £1000 fine – a mere bagatelle for the likes of Acid Jack.

On hearing the announcement of this total travesty of justice, the bereaved widower sprang to his feet and gave uncontrolled vent to his feelings. He ended his tirade by reminding the now grinning Jack with the enigmatic pronouncement that those that choose to live by the sword usually die by the same method.

Jack realized that it had been a close-run thing and without the redoubtable services of Sir Archibald the outcome of the case could have been dramatically different and that he could have been staring at those four prison walls for a far greater period than the paltry 28 days that he had received. But that was now behind him and with his sentence duly served, Jack had now turned into the drive of his palatial homestead. The consolation he now desired more than anything else was to pour himself a long cold beer to be followed by washing away the trials and tribulations of his enforced incarceration by diving into the Hollywood style swimming pool and allowing the cool waters to restore him to a feeling of normality.

He garaged the Lamborghini and quickly divested himself of his clothes. He considered donning swimwear and just as swiftly dismissed the thought. He was on his own private and secluded estate with no prying eyes to catch him 'skinny dipping'. With effortless ease, he scaled the steps of the ten-metre diving board. With a cry of jubilation, he sprang from the board. It was a perfectly executed swallow dive and he could hardly wait for the cooling waters to wash over him. He was barely inches from entering the contents of the pool when he detected a once familiar aroma – It was that of almonds – bitter almonds.

Hidden Talents!

Charles Parkinson was one of life's dyed-in-the-wool sceptics. He doubted everything he was either told or read about until he had personally seen or experienced the incident. If someone said it was two o'clock he would first check his watch to ensure the statement was correct. If informed it was Tuesday he would check the calendar just to make sure and as for some of the 'Strange but True' stories that occasionally appeared in his daily newspaper, after reading them he would without fail let out one of his infamous loud 'harrumphs', which would often cause Mrs Parkinson, who was equally suspicious of the world around her, to drop a stitch.

Charles was also a creature of habit and a great believer in a regular and disciplined routine. After returning from work each day he would consume his tea in silence, check the barometer in the hall, don his coat and trilby, give Mrs Parkinson a perfunctory peck on the cheek before stepping out for his evening stroll.

After 20 years, his route had never varied and it had always concluded down a narrow path through a somewhat secluded wooded area less than a couple of hundred metres from his neat semi-detached bungalow. On that Friday night; the night when it had all begun, Charles's route had been no different. As he passed into the wooded area as usual, he paused to re-light his pipe and threw the spent match into the undergrowth.

"I hope that match was out," came an authoritative voice from nearby. Charles was somewhat startled as he seldom met anybody on this part of his walk and he looked around to ascertain the owner of the rather terse comment – But there was nobody in sight other than a rather scruffy mutt that was sitting just off the path under a large and leafy oak tree. Charles continued to search around the little wood to assure the owner of the commanding voice that the match was indeed out, but search as he did he could find no sign of a fellow human.

"That's how fires start Mr Parkinson and you should know better." Although he still could not identify the owner of the voice, he found himself responding to the admonishment made.

"If you would show yourself sir then I would assure you that the match was definitely out and posed no pyrotechnic problems."

"I am not a 'sir'; my name is Patch," came the immediate response, "And I'm right here in front of you." Charles stared steadfastly at the tree, but there was not a soul to be seen other than the dog that now held him in a steely gaze.

Charles refused at first to accept that the dog had spoken to him. He had heard the spurious claims of besotted owners who believed that they could communicate with their pets but to hear one actually speak – well that was just beyond the realms of credibility. Charles looked behind the tree convinced that someone was pulling some sort of practical joke – But there was no one there.

"I bet you enjoyed those pork chops you had for tea tonight," continued the voice. "I was tied up outside the butcher's shop when I heard Mrs Parkinson ordering them; I had to settle for a marrow bone but I'm not complaining. My master does his best with his job seekers allowance but it sure doesn't run to pork chops – not for me anyway."

Charles's heart was now beating twenty to the dozen. All his life he had refused to believe anything that he had not witnessed for himself and yet now he was beginning to doubt his own sanity. He kept repeating to himself that this couldn't happen – dogs just do not talk – they bark and growl, but talk – Never!

"I bet you think your hearing things Mr Parkinson don't you, but it's true. It's me, Patch, I live with my master Tommy Brown just two streets away from you and often see you walking past." Realization was beginning to dawn in Charles Parkinson's brain and he could no longer doubt the evidence of his own eyes and ears and curiosity, not surprisingly, got the better of him.

"How come you are able to talk?" enquired an almost convinced Charles. "It must be a miracle of some kind I guess."

"Well I suppose you could call it that and if only I could chew on them pork chop bones of yours then I might just be inclined to tell you the whole story – Any chance old boy?" continued Patch with a lean and hungry look in his big brown eyes.

Charles took the hint and hurried the hundred or so metres to where the waste bins were neatly stacked at the rear of his property. Clutching the bag into which His wife had disposed of the bones, he scurried back to the wood to find Patch still there, waiting expectantly. It was not long before the juicy bones were picked clean, a situation which found Charles urging Patch to relate his tale in detail.

"It was about a year ago, when I came here to play with the pixies," began Patch. "Only to find that Twinkletoes, the daughter of the pixie king had been abducted by a gang of nasty gnomes." It was at this point that Charles shook his head in total disbelief of what he was hearing. All his senses were telling him that this was utter rubbish, yet he was so intrigued with such an implausible story that he urged Patch to continue.

"There was only one thing we could do and that was to seek help from the elf army in a supreme effort to save poor little Twinkletoes." Patch paused, and looked beseechingly at Charles hoping that there just might be a few more bones available but realizing that it was a forlorn hope he licked his lips and continued with his tale.

"The ensuing battle was fierce and bloody and for a moment it appeared that the gnomes would win the day. They had Elvis, an elvish princeling cornered and were about to tear him limb from limb when I dashed into the fray. All my terrier training came flooding back and one by one I grabbed the warlike gnomes and shook them hard until there was no fight left in them. The last one I grabbed was a gnomish general and fearing for his life he ordered his companions to lay down their arms and return Twinkletoes to the tender care of her father. His gratitude knew no bounds and he granted me one wish; ye I know what you're thinking, shouldn't that be three? Well let me tell you Mr Parkinson, you mustn't believe all you hear," Charles shook his head in total agreement.

"It's all about hierarchy you know; only fairies and genies can grant three wishes, the lower orders have to settle for the one. I thought long and hard about what to wish for. If I'd had three I would have gone for an endless supply of bones and a diamond studded collar. In the end, I decided to go for the power of human speech so that I could thank Tommy for looking after me so well. Of course, the pixie king granted my wish and as they say, the rest is history."

It was as if a lifetime of mistrust and disbelief were suddenly dispelled from Charles's heart and brain – and it had taken a talking dog to remove the scales from his eyes. No longer would he harbour doubts about the unknown. The previously locked and bolted door to his narrow-minded consciousness had now been flung wide open as he realized that the world did include such fantastical beings like pixies, elves, gnomes and fairies as well as dogs who could hold one in meaningful conversations.

It was at this point when the first little self-doubts began to surface. Was this nothing more than an illusion, brought on perhaps by a dodgy meal (those pork chops had tasted a bit funny)? Perhaps it was the onset of dementia (hadn't he forgotten his wife's birthday last month) or maybe just a trick of the light? There was only one way to solve this dilemma and that was to let someone else hear the dog talking. His mind made up he raced back to his bungalow, grabbed his startled wife by the hand before explaining breathlessly,
"Doris, you just have to come and see this, it's truly amazing…."

Patch was sitting in the same spot under the tree as the couple approached. He looked up at the newcomer and said,
"Hi Mrs Parkinson, how ya doing?" Mrs Parkinson let out a little moan before flinging her pinny over her head and ran screaming from the wood – Charles, was satisfied; this had not been an illusion and he was not dreaming. With a satisfied smile, he followed his terrified wife home, determined to read up on other mysteries such as ghosts, unicorns and pots of gold at the end of the rainbow…….

There was a rustling of leaves as Tommy Brown lowered himself from the tree. He patted Patch affectionally before announcing,
"If I can fool old 'Parky' and his missus with my ventriloquist skills then I reckon the great British public

will be a doddle. Come on old boy, let's go home and dig out that 'Britain's Got Talent' entry form!"

It's a Jesus Thing?

When Wayne finally returned to the land of the living he found himself propped up in a neat white sheeted hospital bed. He knew it was a hospital as he was surrounded and plugged into all manner of high tech' and sophisticated medical equipment. As his heavily bandaged head gradually cleared he realized he was not alone. For as well as the pretty nurse who hovered anxiously over him, there were also three very serious and grim-looking men. Now Wayne had been on the wrong side of the law long enough to realize exactly who these men were. Indeed, it was so obvious to him that they might as well have had CID tattooed on their foreheads.

Wayne was what you might describe as a professional and highly successful career criminal. He had served his illicit apprenticeship at Grimsdale County High School, nicking of any pupil or teacher who were careless enough to leave their belongings unattended. He had then matriculated at the local 6th form college where his specialty had been stealing laptops, ipads and tablets from his unsuspecting colleagues and flogging them via his other dodgy connections. He had finally graduated with honours to house and business burglary at the tender age of 19.

Now although Wayne was a rather unscrupulous and despicable criminal he was without doubt a damn good one. The 'boys in blue' believed that he was probably responsible for most of the crime in the local area, yet despite many close shaves he had never actually been apprehended or charged with any offence. He had been 'brought in' and questioned on several occasions at the local police station but due to meticulous planning he had always managed to wriggle free of being charged and had never ever been caught in the act – until now that is.

There had been some near episodes over the years. Such as the time when he had managed to sneak aboard a well-known millionaire's yacht with the intention of stealing the many jewelled baubles that the cheating cad had showered on his mistress. With the booty in hand he had been rudely disturbed by the unexpected return of the couple. Fortunately, an empty storage locker was to hand in which he had hidden until the amorous duo became involved in activities that had allowed him to slip away unnoticed. As it happened, this had proved not too difficult as under the circumstances he reckoned that a herd of elephants could have thundered by undetected.

Then there was the time when he had stolen the Mayor of Grimsdale's ceremonial chain of office; a gold and silver affair that turned out to be worth more than 30 grand. He had posed as a security guard at the grand opening of the town's new public baths and had obligingly relieved the Mayor of his chain while he became the first person to dip his toe into the water. Unfortunately, he was recognized by one of his ex-teachers who had been the victim of one of Wayne's earlier heists. Realizing he had been 'sussed' he managed to cause a diversion by pushing the Mayor in at the deep end. The commotion that ensued was enough for him to flee the scene, gold chain in hand and an unbreakable alibi already prepared.

Similar 'skin of the teeth' escapes had ensued over the years and it was inevitable that one day his run of good fortune would desert him – and this was destined to be that day. There was no doubt that during his latest break-in Wayne had been the victim of a savage and vicious assault. He was a pitiful figure lying there, encased in bandages from head to toe; a testament to the obvious over reaction from his assailant. Physically he was undoubtedly in poor shape but mentally he was as alert as ever. He knew he had to be and though it was highly unlikely that he would succeed in convincing the officers of his total innocence he needed a plausible story in an effort to escape the full processes of the law, which in Wayne's case were long overdue.

The largest of the three constabulary men was the first to speak.

"Well Wayne, you certainly had a good run for your money but unfortunately your luck has deserted you. Perhaps you can tell us how we came to find you, covered in blood, crawling out of the house you were about to ransack?"

"Well guys, I guess you got me bang to rights, but then again I blame it all on Jesus."

"I've heard some strange excuses for criminal behaviour Wayne but I reckon that tops the lot," said the second policeman shaking his head.

"You gonna tell us he was your accomplice?" continued the third. "Hid the loot in his flowing robes, did he?" he added with a scornful laugh.

"No – no, it was nothing like that. He was the one that attacked me, leaving me in this sorry mess," said Wayne with a sigh.

"Come off it man. That's not Jesus' style. He'd be more likely to turn the other cheek now wouldn't he?" said the big cop, fast losing patience with the forlorn looking figure in the bed, making such pathetic excuses for his nefarious actions.

"It's true – every word of it. If it hadn't been for Jesus I'd have got clean away with the loot and you lot would have been none the wiser," replied Wayne sullenly. "Look, let me tell you how it happened.

I'd done my homework on the house and its occupants, or so I thought. I'd even managed to wheedle the situation of the wall safe out of his cleaner. It's amazing what information some people will reveal for a few 'bevvies' and a curry to follow. The guy was to receive a 'Business Man of the Year' Award that evening and would be accompanied by all members of his family. I knew the premises would be empty for at least four or five hours, giving me plenty of time to be in and out before their return. The house had a good security system but for me getting in was a piece of cake. I immediately made my way to the study where I knew the wall safe was located. I was half way to cracking the entry code when I first heard the voice – It was eerie and the blood froze in my veins. *"Jesus knows you're here!"* it proclaimed. I quickly turned off my flashlight; my heart was beating madly as I tried to make sense of the situation. After all there should have been no one here. It was a minute or so later that I managed to convince myself it was all in my head and that I had imagined hearing the voice and so I resumed my task with the safe. I was one digit from cracking it when once again that same voice proclaimed,

"Jesus is watching you!" This time I shone the torch around hoping to locate whoever was trying to spook me. At first my frantic search revealed nothing and I began to imagine that this really was a holy warning from on high in an effort to persuade me to forsake my wicked ways. It was then that I realized that the voice had actually come from on high and so directed the flashlight's beam towards the ceiling.

   Imagine my surprise, not to say relief when perched high on the light fitting the beam revealed – a brightly feathered and garrulous parrot.

"Was that you speaking just then about Jesus watching me?" I asked rather stupidly. Yeh! I know that parrots are reckoned to be clever birds but hardly able to hold a human in an actual conversation. Turned out I was wrong. This parrot was definitely the exception to its species. I realized this when it replied gravely,

"Of course, it was and I have to warn you that Jesus is still watching you and he is getting very angry." By now I was somewhat relieved when I realized that my adversary was

nothing more threatening than a bird – a clever one no doubt, but still only a bird whose only threat it carried was the distinct possibility of talking me to death with its extensive vocabulary.

With my courage partly restored I laughingly asked, 'Well Polly your religiously motivated threats don't frighten me – I'm an atheist through and through,' and so I continued with my task of opening the safe.

"I'm not called Polly," replied the bird petulantly. "I'll have you know, my name is Moses and I must warn you again that Jesus is now getting very - very angry with you."

"Moses!" I hooted, "What sort of an idiotic owner would ever call a parrot Moses?" With a wicked cackle, the wily old bird replied,

"The same sort of idiotic owner who would call a 140lb Rottweiler Jesus!" – I reckon you know the rest!

<u>The Holiday That Went With a Bang!</u>

"That's it! I've had enough. Another crap day at the office; it seems like I can't do anything right for that pig of a boss," declared Pete as he stormed into the kitchen, hurling his briefcase into the furthest corner of the room. Sue was not overly surprised as this had been Pete's mood for the past few weeks.

"Poor you," she replied in mock sympathy, "And my day at school with a couple of dozen crazy kids to watch over has been a complete bed of roses," she continued with more than a touch of sarcasm in her voice. Jess, who was sat at the breakfast bar, putting the finishing touches to her CV, smiled at the barbed verbal exchanges between her parents before adding,

"I think we all need a holiday – and soon." Pete turned to his 19-year-old daughter and exclaimed with delight,

"Jess, you're not just a pretty face, you've got your dad's brains as well. That's the best idea you've had in ages. I'll bring some brochures home tomorrow." Jess's smile widened as she replied,

"No need dad I know just where we should go – Porto Santo. You want some peace and quiet to recharge your batteries and mum wants the same to make a start on that story she's been threatening to write for months." However, she diplomatically left out the reason why she wanted to visit this little oasis of calm in the Atlantic Ocean with a reputation of having the hunkiest guys in the whole of Portugal. Besides what was running through her mind was not the sort of stuff you would wish to share with your parents, however broadminded they may appear to be.......

Three weeks later the family trio were lounging around the pool of one of the swankiest hotels on the little Portuguese island of Porto Santo.

"If you'd have said a month ago, that I would have been sat around a superb swimming pool in the tropics, ice cold beer in my hand with my two best girls for company, then I would have laughed at you."

"Not quite the tropics dad," replied Jess as she took another sip of her 'Tequila Sunrise.' "But close enough I suppose. Fancy a dip in the pool?" she added turning to her mum. Sue was lying on her tummy, chewing at the end of her pencil and staring intently at the almost blank foolscap page in front of her.

"Not just now Jess," Sue responded, her brow furrowed by the lack of ideas for the story that she was attempting to write.

"Not to worry mum." Said Jess encouragingly, "It's early days yet. There's sure to be something exciting happening soon for you to write about," she added more in hope than expectation as she gazed around at the tranquil surroundings of the lush but oh so quiet resort. "Think I'll stroll over to the poolside bar and try 'Sex on the Beach', she said nonchalantly with a wicked twinkle in her eye.

"Not on my watch young lady you won't," hollered Pete, slopping the contents of his almost empty glass down his front.

"Chill dad," she laughed, "It's a cocktail; not what you're thinking you naughty boy." All three giggled at Pete's apparent lack of knowledge on the cocktail front; a giggle that turned into gales of laughter as he added "If that's the case then I reckon we should all partake then."

"No let me go," said Sue with a resigned sigh. "I might come up with some ideas for this story I'm supposed to be writing with a change of scenery." Sue picked up a tray from the poolside table and made her way over to the well-stocked bar. As she waited for Mario the bartender to mix the cocktails she could not help but overhear a conversation that was taking place behind the low wall that separated the bar frontage from the somewhat secluded outdoor lounge area.

"When does he arrive?" whispered voice number one from behind the wall. "Tomorrow on the noon flight from Lisbon," answered his companion in equally hushed tones. "Is everything in place for his big surprise?" continued first voice. "Oh yes, we have prepared everything well in advance. At 7-00pm tomorrow evening as we take our pre-dinner drinks round the pool I will press the concealed button. Imagine his surprise when the first one goes off – Boom!" The two conspirators rose from their seats and smiled and nodded in friendly fashion as they passed her by. To a casual observer, Sue still appeared at ease and nonchalant on the outside but on the inside her heart was beating like a runaway trip hammer.

To say that she was a little surprised at the content of this somewhat furtive conversation would have been an understatement. In fact she was quite alarmed. Her vivid imagination went into overdrive as she envisaged the arrival of some notable personage to the hotel who was about to be assassinated – by a bomb. Keep calm girl, she muttered to herself. It could be something and nothing.

A rather pensive Sue returned with the drinks and after setting them down announced to Pete and Jess, "I'll be back in a few minutes." She made her way to the front desk and enquired of the concierge if anyone famous was about to visit the hotel tomorrow. The poor man's face paled visibly as he replied, "How do know about that? It is supposed to be top secret. If I tell you then you must swear that you will tell no one else." Sue nodded her assent as the concierge continued in hushed tones. "The president of Portugal is arriving in the morning and will be staying here incognito for a few days in readiness for a very important announcement he will be making to the UN next month – but I repeat, you must say nothing. If news of his visit leaks out, then heads will surely roll.

It all began to make sense to Sue. The president was about to make some important announcement and his opponents were planning to kill him off before he had the chance – and she was the only person who knew of this dastardly plot; the only person who could save him from being blown to smithereens by his enemies.

But how was she supposed to handle this dicey situation. Who, if anyone, could she confide in? Not knowing who was friend or enemy she decided to say nothing – not even to Pete and Jess who were sure to press the panic button and allow the conspirators to escape rather than face the consequence of their dastardly plot. She decided to wait until the following evening and just before the allotted hour she would raise the alarm and the president's bodyguards would do the rest. She imagined that for her timely intervention she would probably be given the freedom of Portugal – or at least a free holiday........

It was 6-45pm the following evening when Sue finally left her room to join her family around the pool. A last-minute change to her choice of what to wear for what promised to be a very exciting evening had put her somewhat behind the planned schedule. However, no need to worry yet, there was still plenty of time to execute her rather neat and cunning plan. As she passed the low wall where she had first heard the plot being hatched, a swarthy hand reached out and grabbed her arm. "Ah! My dearest senhorita, long I have waited for this chance to be alone with you. I have never been able to resist the charms of flame haired women like you – please grant me just one little kiss?"

"Gerroffme," screamed Sue as she tore at the hand that had grabbed her so roughly. With a startled gasp, she realized that her assailant was one of the two men who had planned the president's assassination. Somehow, they had got wind of her scheme and where now attempting to prevent her raising the alarm. She swung her heavy bag at her over amorous assailant, knocking him to the floor before adding, "and I'm spoken for anyway you perv'."

She ran as quickly as her heels would allow, glancing with growing concern at her watch just as the hands showed that the appointed hour had arrived. The second of the two conspirators reached under the table and pressed the concealed button – Her heart did a nose dive as she realized that despite her heroic effort she was too late.......

BOOM! Went the initial loud firecracker quickly followed by a dazzling burst of red, blues and greens from the array of roman candles around the poolside. A flurry of rockets lit up the darkening sky halting Sue in her tracks. Her erstwhile attacker once again caught up with her, offering profuse apologies for his earlier unseemly behaviour. "Forgive me senhora, We Portuguese are sometimes much too impulsive for our own good. I mistook you for your beautiful daughter as you are so much alike you could easily be mistaken for sisters."

"Flattery will get you anywhere you randy rogue," replied Sue with some relief. "But when I heard you talking yesterday with your friend I thought you were plotting to blow up the president."

"Oh, no senhora, he is our uncle and we planned this special firework display as today is his birthday." Sue laughed out loud. "Well there goes my chance of a 'gong' but at least I've got enough material now for a good story – Now where's my pad and pencil?"

Joe's Nativity

It was mid-November and things were hotting up down at St Stephen's C of E primary school. The headmaster had announced at assembly that morning that Miss Shorthouse, the English teacher, who's many duties included organizing and directing the school's performing art productions, would be selecting the cast for this year's prestigious Christmas Nativity play.

For several years now there had been a great rivalry between St Stephen's and the local Methodist school just up the road as to which of them could produce the best Nativity play. Up to now, the Methodist school had been adjudged to stage the most lavish production, but this year Miss Shorthouse was more determined than ever to wrest the Nativity crown from their hands.

To this end, she had enlisted the help of the local amateur dramatic society, who had promised to build a stupendous set that they were confident no other school could rival. With the addition of the society's lighting equipment, Miss Shorthouse had convinced herself that 2 out of 3 of the requisites for an unbeatable dramatic production had been achieved; all she needed now was to ensure that the cast for the Nativity play consisted of the best thespians that the school had to offer.......

Joe Shepherd was fed up. For the past three years, he had auditioned for a part in the Nativity and the good news was that he had always been successful in securing a role; the bad news was that it had always been to play the part of a shepherd. As Miss Shorthouse had said (ad nauseam) at every audition, 'well what do you expect with a name like yours?' to be followed by an ear-splitting cackle that never failed to set Joe's teeth on edge. However, Joe was determined that this year it would be different.......

All the principal roles had been cast apart from one. Up to now, Miss Shorthouse had been extremely satisfied with her choices. Mary was demure with dimples that would melt the hardest hearts. The 3 wise men looked every inch like kings despite their youthful years. The shepherds all had that pastoral appearance about them and looked as though they had spent a lifetime in the fields (Joe had kept a low profile when the shepherd's roles were being cast), yet nowhere among all the children in the school could she spot a boy that would make a convincing and acceptable Joseph.

Joe sensed that Miss Shorthouse was struggling to find what everyone accepted was the leading male role in the sea of eager faces gazing hopefully in her direction – Joe spied his chance.

"Please Miss, I know who would make a good Joseph."
Miss Shorthouse peered suspiciously at Joe over the rim
of her horn-rimmed glasses.

"So pray tell us who in your opinion could possibly fill this
most important role?" she replied with more than a hint
of sarcasm in her voice.

"ME!" Answered Joe proudly. Miss Shorthouse was
somewhat taken aback by this confident response.

"So, tell me Joe, what makes you think that you would
make a good husband for Mary?"

"Well, I may be a 'Shepherd' Miss but I'm also a 'Joseph'.
Not only that but I got top marks in woodwork last term
and I can ride a donkey on Blackpool beach as good as
anybody." Miss Shorthouse could not help but repress a
smile at this boyish declaration and as there did not
appear to be a more suitable candidate she decided to
cast him in the role – if only for his cheek....

Joe threw himself into the part and was always first to
arrive at all the rehearsals. As the weeks progressed, Miss
Shorthouse had come to realize that Joe was turning out
to be an excellent choice for the role of Joseph and her
expectations of getting one over the Methodist school
was growing by the hour. It was such a pity that at the
final dress rehearsal, poor Joe tripped over a shepherd's
crook and broke his leg – There was to be no Nativity play
for him this year!

To say he was disappointed would have been an
understatement. His clumsiness had deprived him of a
starring role and Miss Shorthouse was very much aware
that Joe's understudy, although keen enough, did not
possess Joe's natural acting ability. Her dreams of stealing

the Nativity crown from the Methodist school were now only of the 'pipe' variety....

It was the eve of the opening performance. Joe had been in bed for an hour or so but sleep would not come. All he could think about was tomorrow's Nativity performance that he could neither appear in or even see due to his broken limb – It was then that he noticed a small blue light at the end of the bed that was growing both in size and brightness. It began to move slowly towards him before coming to a sudden halt. There was a distinct 'pop' and like a bubble bursting the light suddenly vanished and in its place hovered a tiny creature dressed all in white vestments with wings on its back and a halo around its head.

"A-a-are you a fairy?" stammered Joe, gazing apprehensively at his uninvited guest.

"Do I look like a fairy?" replied the apparition grumpily.

"Well you do a little bit," responded Joe looking a little more closely.

"Well I'm not! I'm your guardian angel and the boss has sent me to try and cheer you up, so what will it be then, a top of the range iPhone, the latest X box with a selection of all the top games or perhaps a season ticket for Preston North End?". Joe rubbed his eyes and stared unbelievingly at the little figure.

"What I'd really like is to be performing in the Nativity play or if you can't manage that Mr Angel then at least a front row seat at the opening performance tomorrow night."

"For starters, young master Shepherd, I'm not a Mr or a Miss or even an Ms; we angels are all of neutral gender –

it saves a lot of bother up there. If you must you can call me GA and as for your wishes, I could grant either of them with ease. However, I've got something a little more special in mind that may just put a smile back onto your glum looking face – Now how would you like to be present at the very first Nativity?" Joe began to laugh uproariously at this suggestion.

"That happened over 2,000 years ago; you can't travel backwards in time – can you?"
"Backwards, forwards, sideways, any direction you desire; please remember who you're talking to young man and of the powers we angels possess." Joe wondered how anyone could move sideways in time but decided for the moment to keep his council.
"Well I suppose that would be something to talk about in school, but then again nobody would believe me," Joe mused. The angel was now tapping his white satin shoe impatiently. "Oh, what the heck, I don't care if they don't believe me - let's go for it GA....

There was a great whooshing sound and before he had time to catch his breath Joe found himself perched high up in the rafters of a dimly lit stable but he was not alone up there. To his left was an array of wild birds. To his right was a speckled hen accompanied by her chicks. The scene below was breath-taking. There was Mary singing softly to the baby in the manger. Joseph was by her side holding a lamb and three very grand looking gentlemen, each carrying an ornately carved casket, had just entered the stable.

Joe was totally mesmerized at the sight. Everything was as he had been led to believe – even down to the lowing of the cattle, which appeared to have no effect on the sleeping baby – everything that is except for all the birds that were perched with him on the rafters. He would certainly enjoy informing Miss Shorthouse about this omission.

As he turned in the direction of the speckled hen, he slipped on the narrow rafter and felt himself falling. In despair, he reached out towards the hen, grabbing it by its tail feathers – but it was to no avail. He was hurtling down and to his horror he realized that he was about to fall directly onto the sleeping child in the manger....

Joe awoke with a start. Sheets and blankets were all around him and as his head slowly cleared he realized that he had fallen out of his own bed. The last thing he remembered was watching the Nativity perched high in the rafters, accompanied by a host of birds. He recalled falling from the beam and then – nothing. He chuckled to himself as he realized that it had all been nothing but a dream; a lovely dream no doubt but hardly the real thing; that was beyond the realms of credibility –

So why on earth was he grasping so tightly a cluster of speckled feathers in his right hand - and whose was that little yellow head peering out of the tumbled bedclothes going 'cheep'?

The Camels are Coming!

Brian's first holiday abroad was one that he was never likely to forget. After years of alternating between Southport and Blackpool for their annual vacation, Cyril and Hilda Rowbottom, Brian's mum and dad, finally decided to broaden their horizons and visit pastures new. Now you would have expected first time flyers like the Rowbottoms to opt for tried and trusted destinations such as Benidorm or Lloret de Mar – but no! Cyril had been fascinated by all things Egyptian, ever since as a rather naïve 12-year-old his Uncle Billy had presented him with a rather grubby length of bandage, informing him with a solemn face that it was the end of the very roll that had been used to wrap up the mummy of King Tut'. As the years passed, Cyril had become a little more streetwise and had eventually realized that Uncle Billy had been pulling his leg. This had been confirmed when a closer inspection of the bandage had revealed a stamped inscription that was certainly not hierographic but rather bold roman face announcing that the article was 'Property of Preston Royal Infirmary'.

However, the damage had been done and ever since he had received the dubious gift from Uncle Billy, he just couldn't get enough of ancient Egyptian culture and had made a solemn promise to himself that one day he would visit the Valley of Kings and see for himself the sphinx, the pyramids and the final resting places of his beloved Pharos.

Hilda had definite reservations regarding Cyril's holiday choice. As far as she was concerned, Egypt was full of sand, flies and foreigners and had convinced herself that once there she would never be able to get a half decent cup of tea. But there was no dissuading Cyril; his mind was very firmly made up, it was Egypt or nothing. Hilda let out a great sigh of forced resignation but was careful to ensure that her suitcase contained a goodly supply of PG teabags......

14-year-old Brian was bored. They had been in Egypt now for over a week and had visited all the usual tourist spots. Cyril just couldn't get enough of the ancient culture but in Brian's book if you've seen one pyramid or mummy then you've seen them all; Oh, how he longed for a kick-about with his mates on the local rec' or a trip to the local cinema where, with a bit of luck, he might just have bumped into Betty Barnesfather again. Instead he was destined to stay for at least another couple of days in a somewhat seedy hotel, situated in a less salubrious quarter of old Cairo.

When he learned that dad had booked yet another excursion to gaze on even more boring antiquities, along with his mum he rebelled.

"You go and have a good look at Rameses' ring dear" (Brian sniggered), "Me and Brian will go and do a bit of shopping down at the bazaar, we need to take some knick-knacks back with us just to prove we've been." Brian frowned; shopping was not high on his list of things to do but after a little thought he reckoned that anything was better than staring at some old ring, no matter how ancient it was....

While mum was making her mind up between a gaudy statuette of Cleopatra and a copper replica of the Sphynx (the made in Bradford stamp on the underside was barely legible), Brian wandered off down a little dusty alley, lured by the sound of a softly playing musical pipe. As he reached the far end of the alley, the pipe player was revealed. It was an old woman, who on first appearance could have stepped right out of her own mummy case. As Brian came into sight, the aged crone stopped her playing and gave him a toothless smile whilst beckoning him to approach her. As he came to her side, she reached up and took his hand and gazed intently on his upturned palm.

Brian was somewhat startled at what happened next. Speaking in broken English, she informed him that the letter 'C' would play a big part in the rest of his. He would take up a career starting with that letter, the name of his future wife would begin with C and this same letter would bring him great fortune in the years to come. It was then that her face darkened as she lifted her head and howled in great trepidation that the letter would also be the death of him. Her eyes rolled in terror as she screamed out the one word - 'CAMEL'....

Brian had fled from the alley in youthful terror. However, in the cold light of day he realized that what he had heard was all complete bunkum. His career path would take him into the realms of science; If things worked out as he hoped, his life would be shared by little Betty Barnesfather; how on earth the letter C would bring him great fortune he just couldn't imagine and as for camels, he hated the beasts and once he had left Egypt behind he had no intention of ever meeting up with such a bad-tempered creature again...

The first seeds of doubt were sown when, in following a meteoric rise in his chosen career path, he was offered the role of chief research CHEMIST in an international company. The first shoots from the dubious seeds showed themselves as he stood at the altar with a blushing Betty, only to learn that her middle name was CLARISSA, which she hated and never ever used. The fruits from the shoots came almost to maturity when out of the blue he discovered that a long lost Australian relative had died suddenly, leaving his five-million-pound fortune to Brian, his only known relative (Cyril and Hilda had passed away many years previous). Brian was not overly surprised when he learned the name of his benefactor, COLIN CHARLES CARRUTHERS.

The prophecy still caused him some concern and yet the news of his inheritance helped to relegate the thought to the back of his mind.   Further to this his benefactor had stipulated in his will that he and Betty must come to Australia to see for themselves the thriving business empire he had forged in the outback, starting with nothing more than ten Australian dollars, a clutch of platypus eggs and a wide brimmed hat studded with dangling corks...

The ride to the ranch from where Charlie Carruthers operated his business was long, dusty and tiring. The monotony of the journey had been relieved somewhat as Brian and Betty learned from the driver more about the thriving business Charlie had set up, which had been the breeding of endangered indigenous animals such as the platypus and Koala bears. It was only as they were pulling into the compound that Chuck, their chauffeur and manager of the ranch, informed them of the venture that Charlie had been working on just before his untimely demise – breeding humpless camels!!!

Brian's face turned ghastly pale as he digested this little snippet of news. Humpless they may have been but camels they certainly were; it was his worst nightmare coming to prophetic fruition.

"Feisty little buggers they are as well," Chuck informed them. "They certainly did for old Charlie they did; filling their food tray he was when Humpfree, the largest and nastiest of the herd bit him on the bum. Reckon he was never quite the same after that nasty experience. We buried him under the big coolabah tree over there," Chuck added, a pained expression on his sun beaten face.

By now Brian was in a state of near panic. A camel had done for his relative and it was surely now just a matter of time before he was destined to meet a similar fate. His fears became reality when a ranch hand ran over to the four-by-four and informed Chuck breathlessly that Humpfree had once again escaped from the corral and was on the rampage. This was all too much for Brian's ears and with an anguished cry he leapt from the dusty vehicle and just ran – It was a pity that just at that moment an enraged Humpfree rounded the corner of the ranch house and made a beeline in pursuit of poor old Brian. He felt its hot breath on the back of his neck – and he stopped. What was the use of flight; no way on earth could he ever hope to outrun the crazed animal. He dropped to his knees and awaited his fate.

A shot rang out and the camel lay dead at Brian's feet. Chuck came running over carrying the smoking rifle. "He won't bother you any more sir. Guess one of these may calm you down a little," announced Chuck, handing him a pack of cigarettes. Brian accepted it gratefully, lit up, took a huge drag and promptly fell into a fit of coughing from which he never recovered. Betty shed a silent tear as she gently removed the pack from his hand, only to realize the brand she was now holding – CAMEL!

It Could be – Somebody Else!

Lucille loved to shop. Just popping round to the corner shop for a pint of milk gave her a thrill while merely thinking about doing the weekly big shop at the ASCO Supermarket sent her into the realms of near ecstasy that relegated other passions into the 'also ran' bracket.

A visit to ASCO anytime during the year made her deliriously happy but it was during the run up to the Christmas festivities when the real euphoria kicked in. It was a pity that her long-suffering husband Dennis did not share her enthusiasm for retail therapy but after many years of marriage he had just about come to terms with her all-consuming passion which meant that even their annual holiday abroad had to be booked within striking distance of a 'supermercado' or shopping mall....

Sonia Crozier also spent many hours at the ASCO Store, but unlike Lucille hers was most decidedly not a labour of love – she was employed there as a store detective and she hated every minute of her time spent in the store. The problem with being a store detective was that you don't make many friends. You were looked on in a similar fashion as traffic wardens are viewed by motorists or water bailiffs are by sneaky fishermen.

The job by necessity required one to be somewhat of a loner, which at first hadn't sat comfortably with Sonia, as up to starting the job some three years previous she had been an outgoing and friendly people person – but the job had changed her. Where before she had only seen the best in people, she had quickly come to realize that there appeared to be as many rogue shoppers in her home town of Barton Bottoms as there were honest folk in the close-knit community.

However, there was no doubt that Sonia certainly had an aptitude for the job. There was no disputing that she had rapidly developed the knack of spotting a 'wrong 'un' the moment they entered the store. Why, hadn't it been only last week, based on her developing instincts, that she had asked a rather sweet and innocent looking old lady to step into the office and a quick frisk had revealed that the old fashioned voluminous bloomers she was wearing had become a veritable cornucopia of stolen goods that included a leg of lamb, two bottles of brandy and four tins of corned beef, one of which she had launched at Sonia in her frustration at being exposed as a shoplifter that had missed her head by the merest fraction.

She accepted that it was her job to apprehend such miscreants and that sentiment should play no part in its execution, and at one time she would probably have felt a tinge of sympathy for the old dear; thinking that she was probably a lonely old widow getting by on an inadequate pension with very few friends to help her through each trying day. However, in reality, Sonia had since learned that the apparent sweet old lady would generally take her ill-gotten gains to her fence who held court in the 'Old Original Chestnut Tree' each Friday and exchange them for a bag or two of 'weed' which she shared with her sister Ethel over the weekend.

The introduction to the seamier side of life in her home town had hardened Sonia and despite her earlier beliefs that most people were basically honest in their day to day activities, her own heart had hardened to the degree that she was now numbered among the degenerates of Barton Bottoms to the degree that her now callous activities included the abuse of her own position as a store detective by demanding illicit payment from those she had apprehended for shoplifting in return for keeping her mouth shut.

Life at home was no bed of roses either, what with a feckless, workshy husband, Perry and three stroppy teenagers to support, who spent more time on their smart phones than either attending college or seeking employment, Sonia had been tempted on more than one occasion to run off with the milkman who she knew was offering her more than his gold top. Her only relief from this hum-drum lifestyle was her weekly splurge on lottery scratch cards. If the truth be known she spent almost as much on the scratch cards as she did on the family grocery bill...

Lucille was feeling quite exhilarated. Her Christmas shopping trip had been successfully completed and her trolley was overflowing with all manner of festive 'goodies'. Her final call had been to the newspaper and tobacco counter to purchase a book of stamps for the last of her Christmas cards. She joined the little queue behind the lady in the green coat that she had seen in the store many times before, little realizing that this was Sonia, the eagle-eyed store detective.

"And I'll have two dozen lottery scratch cards as well," added Sonia to the assistant as she placed the carton of cigarettes she had bought for her husband in her basket. "Do you ever win anything with those cards?" enquired Lucille curiously. "Well you certainly have a better chance than playing Lotto. I've won lots of small sums but never anything big. I actually won £500 with the first ticket I ever bought and I've been hooked ever since," added Sonia ruefully.
"Come to think of it I did win two prizes at the church tombola last week," exclaimed Lucille, "And they do say that good luck comes in threes, so go on then, I'll risk it," she said as she took possession of her first ever scratch card.

"How do they work?" enquired Lucille as she watched Sonia scratching furiously at her cards. "It's a bit complicated." Sonia replied, "Would you like me to help," she added, spying an opportunity to make some easy cash from this somewhat hapless lottery novice; her own cards had yielded a measly £2 and by the law of lottery averages the 25th consecutive card had a better than reasonable chance of a decent prize. "Wow! Beginners luck indeed, you've won £2 in that first section." Lucille let out a little whoop of delight. The second section revealed nothing. It was as she removed the covering from the third section that the once in a lifetime, heart-stopping moment arrived.

Sonia could not believe her eyes, the symbol £250,000 appeared three times – The jackpot. That amount was more than enough to clear all their debts and set them up for life. She glanced over at Lucille to see her shaking with excitement at the thought of winning a mere £2. 'What would this seemingly rich bitch do with all that money? She probably has enough to live a comfortable life anyway,' she thought to herself – It was at that precise moment that Sonia knew exactly what she had to do...

She handed a card back, but it was not the one that Lucille had purchased. In her excitement, she had not noticed that the card she had been given was one of the 24 that Sonia had purchased, displaying the £2 win while the one with the jackpot was now safely in Sonia's pocket. "What happens now?" asked Lucille of her new-found friend.

"Take it back to the counter and collect your winnings," explained a now smug Sonia, who was already mentally spending her ill-gotten gains. Lucille nodded her thanks and did just that.

As the attendant opened the till there came an almost ear-shattering ringing of bells and sounding of horns all through the supermarket. From around the counter came a beaming and smart-suited gentleman, bearing a magnum of champagne.
"Congratulations madam. I am very pleased to inform you that you are the one millionth customer to come through the ASCO doors and as such you will be richly rewarded with cash and gifts over the next 12 months, which includes holidays for life in a penthouse situated in the south of France, courtesy of our founder Mr ASCO himself. Now what do you think of that?"

As she recovered from the fantastic news, Lucille looked around for Sonia, realizing that if it wasn't for her, this stroke of good fortune would never have happened – But Sonia was nowhere in sight. After informing her boss just where he could stuff the job of store detective, she was now hurrying home to break the good news to Perry and her brood – Oh what times they would have with all that money...

The pair were well into their cups that evening as the ten-o'clock news was broadcast. Lucille and Dennis were, as usual, sipping their nightly mug of cocoa as the solemn-faced newscaster announced that among the other disastrous news of the day, all the current national lottery scratch cards had been declared null and void due to an unexplained printing error...

Lucille sighed resignedly as she released she would have to return the £2 she had won earlier that day...

The Secret Behind The Door!

Joe flung himself recklessly over the roughly stacked pile of decaying logs and landed head first into a huge heap of fallen leaves that thankfully broke his fall. In the distance, he could hear all the usual sounds of a police manhunt; whistles being blown piercingly, the cops shouting to one another incoherently and the dogs baying uncontrollably. There was a time when such activity would have thrilled him, but unfortunately, when you are on the wrong side of the law and you are the man being hunted, the whole process takes on an entirely different concept.

The bank job had gone wrong from the start. What should have been a straight forward surprise hold-up had turned into a complete fiasco. It appeared that their man on the inside had developed last minute 'cold feet' and much to the gang's surprise they found the 'Old Bill' waiting for them as they burst through the bank doors. In the ensuing ruckus, most of the would-be robbers were apprehended; It was lucky for Joe that being the youngest and most nimble of the mob, he had been able to evade capture.

The foiled heist had taken place in a small market town and as Joe fled down the high street and through a maze of alleyways he found himself entering a wooded area on the edge of town. Perfect, he thought to himself as he ran deeper into the undergrowth, knowing that he could probably hide there until the heat died down; little did he realize at that time that the police with tracker dogs were hot on his trail...

He hunkered down among the leaves to catch his breath, knowing that he would need to move on quickly as no doubt the dogs would soon pick up his scent. He looked around, wondering which was the best way to go when he spied the chimney tops of an ancient manor house. Having no better plan in mind he decided to make his way to the house and found it surrounded by a high wall. As he ran around it looking for a place of entry he came across a gate with a sign attached; it read, *'Monks Retreat – Enter all who are weary, for here you will surely find succour.'* Joe had nothing to lose, the sound of the chasing pack was getting louder and he was indeed weary and whoever this 'sucker' was he might just be the guy to give Joe the break he was looking for.

As the gate clanged too behind him, he found himself at the edge of a well-stocked kitchen garden in which several hooded men in grey robes were working diligently. The hooded figure nearest to him looked up from his labours, smiled and enquired of Joe as to how he could help...

It appeared that the inhabitants were monks and that the house was a property attached to the local monastery and it was their allotted task to provide all the vegetables for their fellow monks residing within the monastery. It was fortunate that somehow the manhunt had passed the retreat but it was more of a miracle that Joe had managed somehow to convince the brethren that he was a disillusioned high-flying businessman who craved for nothing more than to leave behind a materialistic world, coupled with a desire to spend the remainder of his days in quiet prayer and solitude. Joe was not exactly thrilled at the prospect of becoming a monk but after much deliberation he realized that it sure beat a 30-year stretch behind bars...

Much to his own surprise, Joe found that the life of a novice monk had its compensations, mainly in the fact that the pressing issues of life outside the monastery confines were now left far behind. These included the gang that were constantly reminding him that if he wished to maintain possession of all ten fingers then it would be wise to settle his gambling debts sooner rather than later; the 'fuzz' that would like to interview him with regards to a recently failed bank job and other heinous crimes in the local area and in particular from Mandy who insisted that the twins she was carrying were definitely his, despite the fact that she was not known as the local 'bike' without just cause.

It was while he was going about his day to day monastic duties that Joe (or Brother Joseph as he was now called) came across the door. It was made of oaken beams bound together by stout iron bands and obviously very old. It looked as though it had not been opened for decades as it was covered in thick dust and innumerable cobwebs. He asked one of his fellow monks as to what lay behind the door. The Brother replied that only those of the inner circle of Brethren were permitted to view what lay behind the door. Apparently, it was so spectacular and breath-taking that those who had been privileged to view the sight were never quite the same again both physically and mentally – And Brother Joseph was suitably intrigued!

After many months of seeking an audience with old Brother Justin, who had been inducted into the inner circle nearly 60-years ago, (longevity was another of the attributes bestowed on those who had seen behind the door) he had finally been granted the privilege. It was in his august presence that Joe was informed of the three tasks that all who sought inclusion within the inner circle were expected to perform before admission was granted and the subsequent viewing of just what lay behind that mysterious door.

Joe took a deep breath as the tasks were revealed to him one by one. It was little wonder that there had been no new members admitted for over 30 years when Joe learned that the first task was to read and memorise the total content of the bible. This task took him 20 years but he achieved it. Secondly, he was handed the complete works of William Shakespeare, with a similar proviso that he read and then commit to memory each play and sonnet before typing out every single word (where was that infinite number of monkeys when you needed them?). It was some 30 years later before he added the final full stop.

All this paled into nothing when he was informed of his final task. He was expected to count all the stars in the visible universe. After a further ten years spent on the monastery roof he realized he was getting nowhere and so he cheated on this one thanks to 'google' and much to the surprise of Brother Justin the final task was achieved in record time.

His daunting mission achieved, Joe was duly inducted into the very exclusive inner circle of monks. There was a great banquet followed by celebrations that lasted for days. Joe, who was now in his nineties, could hardly contain himself as all he had ever wanted from the first day that he had stumbled across the secret door was to find out exactly what lay behind it. Finally, the great moment had arrived and Joe was led to the threshold of the great door and there he was handed a large iron key.

With trembling hands, Joe turned the key in the lock and the massive door swung open. Much to his surprise he discovered that behind the wooden door was another door, this one made of stone. Joe turns humbly to Brother Justin who handed him a key made of bronze that opened the stone door. This time he was faced by a door made from pure silver, to which he was handed a further key, and he opens it, only to find a further door made of ruby. Joe's excitement level mounted. The doors themselves were worth a king's ransom so just what treasures could they be concealing?

He turns once more to Brother Justin, who duly hands him yet another key. Behind that door is yet another door, this one made of sapphire - And so it continued until Joe had passed through doors of emerald, gold, topaz, and diamond. Finally, Brother Justin informs him that this is the last key to the final door. Joe is relieved to know that after many years of completing, what to lesser mortals would be considered virtually impossible tasks, he had finally reached the goal that he has sought over so many years.

He unlocks the door, turns the ornate handle and as the glorious sight is revealed to him he falls to his knees in total and utter wonderment. Never in his wildest dreams could he have imagined being in the presence of something so magnificent, so awe inspiring and so utterly unique. Joe knew even then that his life would never ever be the same again.

Would you like to know what Joe discovered behind that final door? Unfortunately, we can't tell you what it was concealing as you are not an inner circle monk!

The Conductor!

Once upon a time, there was a kid named Alex. Alex was the son of two mega rich parents. When Alex was 6 years old, his parents gave him a toy train. He loved that train, and played with it all day every day. And from that day on he was obsessed with trains. He started collecting model trains and buying everything train related that he could afford. When it was time for him to go off to college, his parents asked him where he wanted to go. "You know what folks, I think I want to go to a train academy and get a PHD in train conducting." (because apparently, you can get a PHD in train conducting in the USA). So, his parents sent him off to the Harvard Academy of Trains, and he spent years and years studying and finally managed to become a fully qualified conductor. All he needed now was a train.

With his shiny new PHD certificate clutched in his hand, Alex went to his parents and sure enough they offered to buy him his first ever train. When they asked him as to what type of train he desired, he replied that he would like a passenger train with an engine made completely out of solid gold. His parents, being mega rich remember, agreed to his request – and so they did. Alex took his train on its first trip across the Midwest until they came to a timber built bridge. Alex wondered if the bridge was strong enough to bear the weight of the train. He got out his conductor's manual, did all the necessary calculations and concluded that if he just travelled slowly then it could just about make it safely across. Unfortunately, his calculations proved to be inaccurate and as the train slowly passed over it, the bridge collapsed. This bridge happened to cross a raging river and all on board died a horrible death on the rocks below, except for one person – Alex, the conductor.

Naturally there was an inquest and Alex was found guilty of murder and was sentenced to be executed by means of the electric chair. The day of his execution arrived and Alex was strapped into the chair and the young executioner flicked the switch. Alex flailed about on the chair and his clothes caught on fire. But letting him die by fire would be cruel and inhuman and so the executioner grabbed a fire extinguisher and put out the fire. Then the doctor was summoned and he checked Alex's pulse to discover that he was still alive! The law was quite clear in these situations and states that a second attempt to execute him is not permitted - and so they had to let him go.

Years passed and Alex went once more to his parents and asks for them to provide him with another train, this time with an engine made of silver because it is lighter and should not cause any further bridges to collapse. On the maiden journey, the train approached Devil's Curve much too fast and it was no surprise when the engine derailed, sending it and the packed carriages into a deep canyon – There were no survivors apart from one – Alex, the conductor.

Once again there is an inquest and once again Alex is found guilty of murder and is sentenced to death by the electric chair. And this time, knowing what happened previously, the executioners used twice the energy as before - But it doesn't work, and so as before, Alex goes free.

Years pass again until one day Alex goes to his parents and asks for another train, this time with an engine made of copper. Everything appears to be going to plan as the train approaches the Cherokee Indian reservation. However, Alex is not paying attention and fails to see the native Indian children playing on the tracks. At the last moment, Alex tries to stop, but he can't and all the poor children are mowed down under the wheels of the massive copper engine.

Alex once more goes to court and is sentenced to death by the electric chair. The executioner is now fully aware that Alex is a hard man to kill and therefore uses twice the voltage for twice the amount of time as with the previous failed attempt - But again it doesn't work and so Alex goes free for the third time.

Once again, the years pass before Alex goes to his parents again and asks for another train, this time with an engine made of aluminium. He takes his train with an aluminium engine down the tracks but fails to notice in front of him, walking unsteadily, is an elderly couple. He tries to stop, but he can't and the elderly couple are killed. So, on this occasion what do you imagine will happen to Alex? Yes, you're right, he goes to court and unsurprisingly is sentenced to death by the electric chair. By now the aging executioner is becoming very frustrated and is determined that this time the murderous conductor will receive his just desserts. He channels all the energy from the entire building and once more pulls the lever. There is a crackle of electric energy, but as the smoke clears, Alex looks a little stunned but is still very much alive and so again he walks away, a free man.

This guy was sure a trier and his parents were not surprised, after more years had elapsed, when Alex visited mum and dad again, but before he can begin his usual request, his father interrupts and pleads with his son to just go for a regular train made from all the usual materials, as he just might have a little more success, besides, their bank manager had recently informed them that they were down to their last billion. Alex gave this proposal some thought before finally agreeing that it was worth a shot.

The maiden trip was trouble free and Alex was so exhilarated by this success that he steamed into the terminus at such a speed that the train ploughed into the buffers and straight through the station café, killing everyone inside. It was no surprise to anyone when Alex was again hauled into court and sentenced to death by the electric chair. The white-haired executioner was ready for him this time and had diverted all the energy from the entire block with the intention of channelling it all into the chair - But it doesn't work, and so Alex goes free

So, in due course, Alex goes to his parents again and knowing how close they are to destitution, asks for another train, this time one made of wood, which is duly built and delivered to him. The first journey appears to be going well and this time Alex keeps a sharp lookout for stray humans on the track. He is so wrapped up in this task that he fails to spot a colony of lemmings crossing the tracks and the wooden train ploughs through the colony, killing them all. Alex believes he will get away with this one as they are not humans and were probably looking for a cliff to hurl themselves off anyway. However, he had underestimated the power of the Animal Rights Activist lobby who insist that this is a heinous crime against the animal kingdom and because of his previous convictions he should stand trial.

And so, and for the fifth time, Alex goes to court, and is sentenced to death by the electric chair. The white-haired and wizened executioner knows that this is probably the last opportunity of turning Alex into a blackened crisp and gets permission from the mayor to use all the energy from the whole city and funnel it into that chair - But it doesn't work, and so Alex goes free!

So, Alex goes to his parents again and begs them for one last train as he is determined to show the world that he is a good conductor, this time he takes possession of one made of recycled rubber. The rubber train speeds down the track on its maiden journey, hits an obstacle and because of its composition, bounces high in the air and comes crashing down onto a bus full of Mexicans who have entered the country illegally and are now being returned to their own country. The bus full of illegal Mexican immigrants are wiped out. Once again Alex is hauled into court, despite a last-minute intervention from President Trump who had recently awarded him the Congressional Medal of Honour for services rendered to his country. The judge however shows little sympathy, being a 'dyed in the wool' Democrat, and sentences Alex to death by the electric chair.

The white-haired, wizened and wheel-chair bound executioner has been hauled out of retirement for this one last job and this time, after reluctant permission from the president, utilizes all the electricity from the western half of the US - But it doesn't work, and Alex is set free.

It was then that a little kid walks into the executioner's room, looks around and says, "I know why it isn't working!" And with his dying breath the executioner asks how he has arrived at that conclusion and the cocky kid says, "Well I reckon it's pretty obvious - He's just a bad conductor!"

I'm Not Sitting There!

Mildred was frustrated, angry and rather tired. She had been up since 5-30am that sunny day in May as she was flying down from New York to Florida on her annual spring vacation. It had been a trying day; first her taxi had arrived late and it had taken ages for it to negotiate the never-ending stream of traffic in downtown Manhattan. Check-in at LaGuardia had been a nightmare, her overweight suitcase had prompted a $50-dollar surcharge and the departure board informed her that the scheduled flight to Miami would be delayed by at least three hours.

Finally, the call came for all passengers to proceed to gate D04 in readiness for boarding. Mildred hurried as fast as her 50-year-old, 5ft, 140lb frame would allow her, yet despite her haste she found herself at the rear of the queue that had now formed at the departure gate. She noted with envy that the handful of first-class passengers were permitted to board first, which made her wonder who her companion would be as her seat was in economy class. A lady of her own age would be nice; somebody with similar tastes that she could engage in girly conversation in order too wile away the dreary hours. A handsome and single male would be something of a bonus; age was immaterial to Mildred as she fancied herself as a bit of a cougar although truth be known she was more likely to be compared with a rather flabby and toothless lioness.

Her reverie was interrupted by the pretty flight attendant informing her that this was her designated seat. She thanked the young lady and was about to take her seat when with horror she realized that the adjacent seat was occupied by a black man, grinning at her like the proverbial Cheshire cat. In disgust, Mildred immediately summoned back the young flight attendant and demanded a new seat. Somewhat perplexed the flight attendant enquired if there was a problem. Mildred replied, "I cannot possibly sit here next to this black man." The now concerned flight attendant, in an effort to defuse what could possibly become an embarrassing situation said, "Let me see if I can find you another seat." After checking, the flight attendant returned and informed Mildred that there were no more empty seats in economy, but that she would check with the captain to see if there was an available seat in first class.

It was about 10 minutes later when the flight attendant returned and told Mildred that the captain had confirmed that although there are no more seats in economy, there is one in first class. She also added that it was the airlines policy to never move a person from economy to first class unless it was due to a dire emergency. He had considered the situation most carefully and had reached the conclusion that being forced to sit next to an unpleasant person did constitute an emergency and as such the captain had agreed to make the switch to first class.

Mildred beamed with a self-satisfied smile and prepared herself to be escorted to the comfort of a first-class seat. It was then that Captain Elijah Xhosa emerged from the flight deck and before Mildred could say anything, he gestured to his fellow black man and said, "Sir, if you would so kindly retrieve your personal items, we would like to move you to the comfort of first class as we would not want you to sit next to an unpleasant and bigoted person."

Be Careful What You Aspire Too!

George Baxter finally regained his senses. He shook his head in a somewhat futile effort to clear his befuddled senses. The last thing he remembered was the huge truck hurtling towards him as he attempted to cross the busy High Street of his home town – and then – nothing.

He gazed despondently around him at the unfamiliar and quite disgusting surroundings. It was as though he was in the poorest quarter of the grimiest city on the planet. George wandered aimlessly along the rubbish strewed streets. Shadowy figures passed him on all sides but none stopped to enquire about his obvious dishevelled state; apart from one tatty looking beggar, who appeared to be in a worse state than George, who stopped and enquired if he was a 'Newbie'. George by now was more puzzled than ever and although his new acquaintance, who he later learned was called Sam, spoke English, he hadn't a clue what he was going on about.

"You're in hell, hades, the bottomless pit, the afterlife, call it what you will" explained Sam, "But you must have been a real bastard when you were alive, because this is the fourth level and only the worst people who ever lived are sent here." George looked closer at the shadowy figures who were still passing and could have sworn that he recognized Adolf Hitler walking by, arm in arm with Attila the Hun.

His reverie was interrupted by the sound of a loud and piercing siren going off. The dreadful noise terrified George but he is pacified when Sam places a friendly arm around his slumped shoulders and calmly leads him to a big, dilapidated warehouse where thousands of other similarly unkempt souls are gathering. George asks Sam why all the people are here and he points to a long line of folding tables against the wall. Each table has stacked on it some mouldy bread, cups of dingy water and bowls of broth so thin they were hardly distinguishable from the water. It was at that point that George realized how hungry he was. A brutal looking guard in heavy body armour then blew a whistle and all the miserable looking people arranged themselves into three lines.

Sam then explained to George that the first line is for the bread, the second is the broth line, and the third was the water line. Sam explains further that all the food here is free, but if you want to get out of this maggot hole, then you've got to work, because the gate guards into the third level demand 500 Euros for an aspiring citizen to move up (Ah! So, we're in the EU somewhere then). Sam added that he had heard it was worth every cent as the food is much better there."

George and Sam sit down to eat their unappetizing food and as expected it was abominable. At that precise moment, George vowed to make the necessary 500 Euros and get himself up to the third level. He took on any menial job he could and despite the lousy rates paid, after ten years of hard graft, eating the mouldy bread and indistinguishable soup and stinky water, George finally saved up the required sum. The guards let him through and he found himself on the third level. It's nothing too fancy, if anything, it's a bit below average for a real city, but in comparison it is paradise. All the guards look much friendlier, and the houses and buildings, while not spacious or lavish, are certainly a step up from those on the fourth level. He had been there less than an hour when much to his surprise, he met up with the familiar figure of his fourth level friend - Sam.

"What are the odds?" they both ask as they shook hands warmly and got to conversing. Sam, it turns out, had only managed to make it in himself a few months earlier. Their conversation was interrupted, however, by what sounded like a school bell. George was confused until Sam led him to what looks like a giant gymnasium. Here, people are gathering once again and George quickly realizes that this is another feeding station. On a line of folding tables against the wall are stacks of hot dogs, big bowls of salad, and huge jugs full of fresh lemonade. A guard shouts for everyone's attention and commands them all to stand in three lines. Sam smiles at his friend's wonder and points to each line in turn. "That's the hot dog line, that's the salad line, and that's the lemonade line." George got into each line in turn and provided himself with a most satisfying lunch.

While George was eating, and basking in joy at not being stuck with old mouldy old bread and minging water, Sam further informed him that there are further benefits to enjoy as halfway through the year, they switch the menu too chicken, chili, and hot chocolate.

Sadly, accepting this routine for eternity proved to be too much as after only a few years, George grew tired of the same meal every day, despite the half-yearly menu change. However, he knew from local gossip that it was possible to change his lot and move up to the second level. This time unfortunately the guards were asking for 10,000 Euros for this change of scenery. George was mortified, but he figured that he had eternity ahead of him now and so he had all the time in the afterlife to save up to achieve his goal.

After 50 years of hard work, he went back to the guards with the requisite money in hand and they allowed him to pass through the gate into the second level where he found himself in a glittering, clean city full of glass and steel; and wouldn't you know it, but there, standing across the street was Sam, only now he was out of his rags and wearing a well-fitted suit. George greeted his old friend and they started talking. Once again, their conversation was interrupted, only this time it was by beautiful church bells. "Come," said Sam, "I'll take you to the evening meal." George followed obediently and the pair entered a glamorous ballroom filled with hungry but well-dressed patrons.

Even the guards here looked good, dressed in suits and sunglasses like bodyguards to the rich and famous. George was not surprised to discover that there were long mahogany tables against the walls, onto which were huge silver platters piled high with cuts of the finest steak, bowls of the most delicious seafood soups and best of all huge magnums of the finest vintage champagnes.

One of the bodyguards cleared his throat loudly and politely requested that the patrons line up. Three lines were formed and Sam pointed to each line out in turn, informing George that the first was the steak line, the second the soup line and the third the champagne line. George was even more pleased when Sam added that they change the menu every month! George rejoiced, he ate until he was full and was deliriously happy and for once felt that nothing was lacking. A fresh menu once a month was most satisfactory to him and he realized that eternity in the afterlife was probably going to be endurable after all.

The next 100 years flew by but humans being humans they often get bored with the same old lifestyle and so one day, out of curiosity, he went up to the guards that patrolled the gate into the first and final level of the afterlife and found they were asking for a 1.000,000 Euros to pass through. Now it's fair to say that George was a little disturbed by this news, "After all," he mused, "How could anything be more wonderful than what I have right here?" The question haunted him for a decade or two until finally he arrived at a conclusion. He was used to working hard and he had all of eternity to save up and he just had to see what he could possibly be missing on the first level. It was 100 years later when he finally returned to the guards with the requisite 1,000,000 Euros.

When George stepped into the first level he fell to his knees. The architecture was glorious and certainly out of this world. The guards, if you wanted to call them that, were all shining angels who bowed as he passed them. To his surprise, someone helped him up off the street and when he looked, he realized who it was--it was Sam, the man he had first met on the fourth level. He was adorned in a golden robe studied with precious stones and when George looked down at himself he realized he was attired in much the same way.

Sam laughed jovially before informing his friend that he had arrived almost three years ago, but somehow had known that George would be close behind him. Suddenly, the air was filled with the sound of angelic choirs and Sam led the man off to a gigantic palace made of crystal and cloud. The room was filled with radiant citizens of the first level and angels prepared everything for them. Sure enough, there was a line of massive altars against one wall, spilling over with glistening golden dragon meat, golden platters filled with angel dust stew and a pudding refined from clouds and dew and silk, smothered in ice-cold tubs of ambrosia and nectar ladled out bountifully into blindingly beautiful crystalline chalices. An angel fluttered from the ceiling and bowed silently to the assembled mass, who bowed respectfully back and then broke themselves into their lines on their own.

Smiling with satisfaction at the tradition, Sam pointed to the first line informing George that this was the line for the dragon meat and the second for angel dust stew while the third was for the ambrosia pudding and nectar wine. On closer inspection George realized that there was a fourth line but there was nobody in it. He wandered over to read the notice that was attached to the adjacent wall; it read as follows: -

Look around and feast your eyes

yet pass through here for a greater prize!

There was an arrow pointing to what one could only describe as celestial gates set in the far wall. George guessed instantly that this was the door that would lead him from a prison, albeit a most comfortable one, into what can only have been paradise itself, where the lifestyle there would be infinitely superior to even this one on the first level.

George made an instant decision. With glazed eyes, he marched steadfastly towards the pearly gates despite warning cries from Sam and the other patrons. He was deaf to their entreaties to change his mind and as he neared them the gates swung open as if to welcome him in. As he passed over the threshold there was a thunderous clap of thunder accompanied by blinding flashes of lightning which temporarily blinded him.

As his vision returned he gazed around and found that – he was back on that same dingy street when he first entered the fourth level. His golden raiment's had disappeared and in their place, were the same old rags that he wore on his first entrance into the hell hole – His blood ran cold.

He heard a wicked cackle behind him and as he turned, expecting to see his old friend Sam but instead he found himself gazing into the blood-red eyes of a terrifying demon.
"Why am I here?" he implored of the satanic figure.
"I thought I was entering the gates of heaven."
"Heaven is not for the likes of you my lad. You had the chance of a better life than this but like all greedy humans you wanted more."
"Am I condemned to spend eternity here then?" George enquired forlornly.
"Nay my son, this place is far too good for the likes of you and your ilk. You will now pass through the final door into your own personal hell," the demon announced, pointing a scaly, long nailed finger towards a decaying wooden door that had now appeared in front of him. With great fear and apprehension mounting in his breast, he passed through and found himself – in downtown Barton Bottoms on a Friday night – Just as the pubs were turning out!

The Man on the Stool!

As Hank Bocholt slouched lazily on the high stool in the dimly lit downtown bar, he sighed audibly before taking another sip of the now warm beer that he had been nursing for the past hour or so. His fellow drinker on an adjacent stool cast an inquisitive eye in the direction of the sigh and enquired,

"You alright old-timer?" Hank turned a rheumy eye in the direction of the voice, looked at the owner with a practised eye and reckoned he was probably worth a beer or two and maybe even a shot of JD.

"Ye I'm getting there I suppose. I was just remembering the time when I shot a man and the judge decided that it was a suicide." The man, like a tenderfoot trout, was hooked at the first cast and moved his stool a little closer.

"Reckon that's the 'Bud' talking," grinned the younger man. "Can't see how that would be possible," he added.

"Well I could tell you more but my mouth is getting a little dry; a little lubrication would help though," Hank responded. The landing net was now out and before he could add to his suggestion, Hank found himself in possession of a freshly pulled glass of the house special. Hank took a long hard swig, wiped the froth from his lips and began his story.

"It was about ten years back now when things were a little easier. I had a good job, money in the bank, a fancy apartment on the 9th floor of a swish tenement block and me and Martha, God rest her soul, wanted for nothing. It hadn't always been easy for us. When we were first married, I was a long-distance trucker and I guess, we spent more time apart than together in those first five years. S'pose it was a blessing when little Herman came along as it gave Martha something to do on those long days and nights when I was on the road.

Well I worked hard and always delivered my cargoes on time and I was eventually made yard foreman. I introduced some new ideas on routes and scheduling that pleased Mr Kaminsky, the owner of the business and when I came up with the slogan 'Let Kaminsky Karry It', well he was so pleased with the extra business that came in that he made me General Manager of the whole fleet and with a salary to match.

Little Herman was growing up fast and I guess we spoiled him a little. Unfortunately, it didn't make him grateful and the more he got the more he wanted. I tried to put my foot down on many occasions but it was Martha who was the soft touch. If I refused his growing demands he just went to his Ma and she would always give in to him.

He was a bright kid but lazy and was only accepted into college because I greased the palm of the dean. He lasted about 18 months before dropping out and became very friendly with a certain Mr Marijuana and his acolytes. Despite Martha's protest, I kicked him out of the house when I found him attempting to break into our little wall safe for the few dollars I kept in there, and all to feed his growing habit. He then joined up with a commune of likeminded dossers and for a couple of years or so we lost touch.

Martha was becoming increasingly tetchy, guess she was missing Herman more than I was. She would fly off the handle for no good reason and the only way I could ever calm her down was to threaten her with 'Betsy', my old shotgun. Now don't get me wrong mister, it was never loaded, I didn't even have any cartridges in the apartment so it was an empty gesture in more ways than one. Whenever she heard the click of the trigger though she would calm down immediately. I certainly wasn't proud of what I was doing but I reckoned that the end justified the means."

Hank paused, glancing expectantly at his near empty glass. The man on the stool took the hint and as the pot was replenished Hank continued with his tale.

"It was about a year after Herman had left to live in the hippy commune when Martha and I arrived home late one night to find we had been burgled. It turned out that Herman and a couple of his shifty pals had turned the place over and gotten away with most of Martha's bling. There was nothing that precious but it really hurt Martha to know that her only son could be so heartless as to rob his own family. Any motherly feelings she may have had for him evaporated faster than the morning mist after the sunrise. First thing she did was cut him out of her will and she took great delight in telling him so. Me? Well I considered it but just couldn't do it. He was our only kid and maybe someday he would realize the folly of his ways and return to the fold. Besides, there was no one else in the frame to benefit from our few thousand bucks, except for the dog's home, and I aint that fond of doggies."

Once again Hank's glass was drained and once again the man on the stool replenished it.

"Somehow or other, Herman got wind of what happened with the wills and I guess that was what prompted him to do what he did next. He obviously figured that if Martha outlived me then there was no chance of him ever getting his mitts on the dough. So, what did he do? The little shit broke in one night and slipped a live cartridge into old 'Betsy', knowing that sooner or later we would have one of our inevitable rows and I would grab the shotgun and go through the motions of shooting her – only this time it would be for real. I would be arrested for murder, given the lethal injection and Herman would inherit enough 'Moola' to keep himself in weed for the rest of his days.

It's funny how woman think but the fact that Herman was now out of her life, Martha calmed down considerably and 'Betsy' lay undisturbed in the cupboard for the next couple of years until that fateful night when the city was enduring one of the sweatiest heatwaves it had ever experienced. Herman's name came up in conversation and ole Martha went ballistic. Reckon I had little choice but to retrieve old 'Betsy', gave her the usual warning, which had no effect, leaving me with little choice but to pull the trigger. The bang that followed scared the Bejasus out of both of us. Luckily the discharge missed her and went harmlessly through the open window – or so we thought until that dreadful pounding on the door of the apartment a couple of hours later – It was the cops! I was cuffed and taken down to the 13th precinct, grilled and charged with homicide...

It appeared that earlier that same evening there had been an attempted suicide. The young guy involved had obviously found that life was too much for him and had decided to hurl himself from the roof of our building to end it all. What he didn't realize was that he would never have succeeded. There was some building work taking place on the top floor and a safety net had been installed in the case of accidents, which would have saved the would-be suicide. Unfortunately for him, he just happened to be hurtling past our window when the shotgun was discharged, blowing his brains out.

Of course, there was a trial and after all the evidence was heard the judge discharged the jury and returned a verdict of suicide." The empty glass was returned to the bar top for the third time and ole Hank just knew that it would be instantly recharged – and so it was, by the man on the stool.

"I've heard some tall tales from beer addled panhandlers the likes of you," scoffed the man on the stool, "But I reckon that one beats the lot. How on earth can you shoot a man dead and the judge declare it a suicide?"

"Well, let me tell you. When all the facts came to life and it was proven that Herman had loaded the gun unbeknown to me, the judges first reaction was to call it 'accidental death'."

"OK, I get that, so how did he arrive at the suicide verdict?"

"Well it appears that the deceased was fed up of waiting for money that was coming to him and so decided to end it all. He succeeded, but not quite in the way he had planned it."

"I still don't get it," said the man on the stool. "Who was this guy anyway?"

"Ah! There's the rub," replied Hank. "Turns out the guy was called Herman – Herman Bocholt – my son. After hearing all this, the judge concluded that as Herman had placed the cartridge in the shotgun that he had actually murdered himself and so closed the case as a suicide." Hank drained his glass.

The man on the stool shook his head in disbelief as Hank lowered himself from his place at the bar and walked unsteadily towards the door, his work for the night satisfactorily concluded. How do I know all this you may ask dear reader? – I was the man on the stool!

Button It Son!

"What on earth has come over you son?" shouted a very concerned father to his only son Alec who was in his first year at the Barton Bottoms Academy of Arts & Science. "Your first academy report is terrible, and you were doing so well before at primary school." Alec hung his head in shame. He knew his dad was right but also knew that unless he got them there was little chance of his school work improving.

"Gee dad, I'm sorry. I know you expect big things from me but I just can't concentrate without them."

"What the blue blazes are you talking about Alec; what are 'them'?" "Assorted brass buttons dad. If you just get me 100 or so I'm sure it will make all the difference and I can guarantee that my academy work will improve by leaps and bounds."

"What the dickens do you want with 100 assorted brass buttons."

"Well it's kinda private dad. All I can tell you is that

without those assorted brass buttons I'm doomed to a life of failure."

Dad was in a quandary; naturally he wanted his son to be a success but he also respected his need for privacy and so he went online, found a specialist clothing company that stocked assorted brass buttons and purchased 100. The effect was miraculous and for the next term or so, Alec began to excel in all subjects – then within days of moving up a class it all went wrong again. A similar conversation took place as before, the outcome being a firm promise to improve if only dad would get him 1000 brass buttons, which of course being a caring parent, he did.

The effect was instantaneous. Within days of receiving the buttons Alec became once more a grade 'A' student in virtually every subject he was studying, that is until he moved up to the next class and was struck once more with unexplained lethargy in the learning stakes. Once again, his father took him to task and once again Alec made the same old plea. "It's just that I worry too much about the brass buttons dad; I'm just not getting enough for my project. I reckon a further 10,000 should do the trick."

With growing reluctance, dad managed to get hold of the requisite number of brass buttons and as before the change that came over his son was nothing short of a miracle. Not only did he excel in his academic subjects but he also became most proficient on the cricket field. He was now at college and his skill with the willow and leather soon attracted the attention of the sports committee.

He was invited to take a 'net' with the other 'possibles' and after launching the first dozen or so balls into an adjoining field some 70 metres distant, his name was immediately added to the team sheet of the first eleven, who at the week-end just happened to be playing their greatest rivals and nemesis, St Chads, a team they had never beaten since W G Grace had graced a cricket field.

Now I imagine you are thinking that Alec, like a resurgent character from 'Vitai Lampada', knocked off the winning runs for his college in true stiff upper lip British style? – Wrong! – he was out first ball. In the pavilion, his father slipped a consoling arm around his shoulder. "What happened old son?" he enquired of Alec sympathetically.
"It's those damned brass buttons again dad. I'm gonna need at least another 100,000 to finish my project; until then I don't think I'll be able to hit another run or bowl another ball," he sighed with a salty tear running down his cheek.

Alec's dad swallowed hard. He was between the proverbial rock and hard place. He dearly wanted his only son to be successful in life but just where was he supposed to obtain 100,000 brass buttons before the return fixture with St Chads next month. It was a struggle but thanks to the internet and the fact that the British armed forces was to be reduced by half, the requisite amount of shiny brass buttons became available and Alec's dad snapped them up at a bargain price.

It was no great surprise to Alec's dad when, thanks to the receipt of the 100,000 brass buttons, his son was the key factor in the total demolition and humiliation of the previously unbeaten St Chad's cricket team. He took 9 wickets for 23 and then knocked off the required runs in the first over. After such a devastating performance, Alec was destined to go down in the annals of college cricket for all time.

Unknown to Alec and his father, there had been a county scout present at the match and he wasted no time in inviting Alec for a trial at the county ground. Alec put in another majestic display at his trial and was immediately offered a generous contract to join the county club as soon as his college studies were completed....

In his first appearance for the county team he bowled four overs and had figures of no wickets for 64 runs and was out first ball when he took up the bat. Once again Alec's father found his son slumped inconsolably in the pavilion sobbing as though his whole world had collapsed. "I'm so sorry dad, I've let you down again and it's the same old problem. I vastly underestimated the number of brass buttons I'd require to complete my project." Dad by now knew that his son had great potential to be a world class cricketer; he also anticipated what would come next. "So how many will it take this time son to get you back on track?"
"Gee dad, I'm not sure there are that many brass buttons in the whole world," sighed Alec despondently. "Though I reckon another 1,000,000 will just about do it," he added imploringly.

Don't ask me how he did it but within a month Alec's dad had somehow managed to collect a million brass buttons and they were duly delivered to the studio that Alec had rented in downtown Barton Bottoms. Needless to say, Alec was over the moon and showed his gratitude by becoming the greatest all-rounder that had ever played for the county. In his first season, he had accumulated 1,000 runs by mid-May and taken over 30 wickets at the unbelievable cost of only 5 runs per wicket.

His rise to fame had been nothing less than meteoric and not a player in the team or a cricket lover in the land were surprised when he received the inevitable call from the England selectors to open the batting for his country against their greatest rivals – the Aussies…!

The fifth and final test match had been keenly contested. The series stood at two victories each and the game was now in its final innings with England chasing a score of 320. They had done well but were now in the final over with 9 wickets down and 23 runs short of passing the Aussie's total. Alec had carried his bat and was just 17 runs short of a double century. Fortunately, he was facing the bowling and realized that the outcome of the whole series and retention of the Ashes rested on his young shoulders. His partner was a demon fast bowler but as a batsman he was rubbish. Somehow, Alec knew he had to retain strike or it would be all over.

The first ball was safely dispatched to the boundary, as were the 2nd, 3rd, while the 4th was sent over the pavilion stand for a majestic 6, which took Alec to his double 'ton'. There were rousing cheers ringing around the packed ground and Alec raised his bat and helmet in acknowledgement of the riotous plaudits – but there was still work to be done. Five more runs were required and it appeared that this would be achieved when Alec once again launched the 5th ball in the direction of the pavilion. However, he had not quite middled it and it appeared to be heading straight to the hands of a fielder just inside the boundary ropes.

"Run," screamed Alec to his partner and much to the delight of the partisan crowd, the fielder caught, juggled somewhat, before he finally dropped the ball and the pair managed to gallop to three runs. England were within two runs of a famous victory with one ball to come, unfortunately the strike was now with Alec's extremely nervous partner. The final ball he received clipped the edge of the bat and just evaded the outstretched hand of first slip. The gallant duo ran as though their lives depended on it.

The scores were tied and it appeared that a further run was impossible – but not in Alec's mindset. He urged his partner to run while he himself sped back down the pitch to the end were the ball would be returned. However, it looked as though the superhuman effort was to be in vain as the ball was hurled with deadly accuracy and speed in the direction of the stumps and appeared to be winning the race. Within five yards of the crease Alec, with bat outstretched, launched himself in the air – right into the path of the speeding ball, which struck him on the temple with a sickening crunch that was heard all over the ground.

He was rushed semi-conscious into the pavilion and lay cradled in his father's arms whilst waiting for the ambulance to arrive.
"Did we do it dad?" he whispered faintly to his distraught father.

"We certainly did son. Your head stopped the ball hitting the stumps and the two runs were awarded." Alec smiled weakly at this news and his eyes dimmed. Father feared the worst, yet even at this trying time he was eaten up with curiosity as to just what his son had done with all those brass buttons. Through tear-filled eyes he posed the question that had been bugging him for many years. "Tell me son, what did you do with all those brass buttons?" Alec raised himself slightly, looked dad in the eye, gave a little cough that brought blood to his lips and.....

Now, dear reader, as this tale is part of a 'Never saw that coming' anthology, I imagine you will be thinking that the next line would probably be; 'Then he died,' – but you would be wrong. Now read on.

And then, though in great pain and discomfort, Alec described to his father how he had melted down the massive collection of brass buttons and then sculpted the resulting ingot into a gigantic brass neck over 10 metres high. Alec's father was impressed though perplexed and asked his son as to the meaning and purpose of such an unusual work of art. Alec informed him that it was to reveal to the world who he, and many others, considered to be the most selfish, arrogant, self-centred person, with the cheek, audacity and over bearing brass neck who believed it to be his right and duty to impose his highly unpopular will on the people.

Alec's dad was very proud of his son for taking on such a selfless and time-consuming project to expose this unquestionable charlatan in such a unique and unforgettable way.

"You are indeed a genius my son and your work will be recognized, revered and accepted the world over, but tell me, which unmitigated and tiresome scoundrel does this 10-metre-high brass neck sculpture represent?" Alec once more raised himself up, looked his father squarely in the eye, opened his mouth as if to speak – **and then he died!**

Yo Ho Ho and All That!

It was the year of our Lord 1717 and Captain Beauregard Templeton, master of the good ship Lionheart out of Boston, scanned the horizon anxiously with his telescope. He was aware that they had entered dangerous waters that were regularly patrolled by the pirate fraternity but to reach their destination he had little choice but to sail this route.

Everything appeared to be in order and he heaved a sigh of relief and began to think that they would reach their destination unmolested, that is until he heard the dreaded cry from the 'crow's nest',

"Sail ahoy, off the starboard bow." The captain once again raised his glass in the direction indicated and sure enough he could just make out the outline of a fast-moving vessel on the horizon – and it appeared to be heading straight for the Lionheart.

It was too soon to panic; perhaps it was another merchant vessel that happened to be sailing on the same course, or maybe even one of His Majesty's frigates, engaged in the duty of hunting down pirates and privateers in these perilous waters. Beauregard comforted himself with these thoughts as he strained his eyes to see what colours the ship was flying. It was less than mile away when he first made out the pennant flying proudly on the mainmast – It was not the dreaded skull and crossbones that all peace-loving mariners feared to see bearing down on them; Oh, no it was far worse than that. It was the effigy of a newly castrated sailor, his face contorted in the agony of his death throes. It was the insignia of a vicious gang of female cutthroats, feared from the Bay of Biscay to the Spanish Main – The Barbary Coast Bitches and led by the wickedest woman who had ever drawn breath – Sinister Sally.

Across the seven seas they had plied their evil pirating trade for six long and bloody years. No merchant vessel was safe from this marauding band of busty buccaneers and their wicked exploits had given a new meaning to the act of rape and pillage as although never a man was spared when a ship was ransacked, the male victims all appeared to have died with huge smiles on their faces (and it was nothing to do with pillaging).

Although Sally was now adjudged to be a heartless monster, this had not always been the case. Up to the age of 18 she had been a shy, demure and attractive girl with Titian tresses that tumbled over her fulsome bosom, reaching down to her slim boyish waist and framing a face of flawless beauty. She was the apple of her father's eye and loved by all who knew and desired her in the little town of Barton Bottoms.

It had been on a family vacation to the seaside when all this had changed dramatically. Sally had decided to go for an early morning swim from the apparently deserted beach and saw no need to wear bathing apparel – This had been a great mistake on her part as anchored close by was a ship of the line and her rash action to bathe naked had been spotted by the eagle-eyed look-out.

The next thing that Sally became aware of was being surrounded and pawed by half a dozen randy sailors. What happened in the following hours I will leave to your own imaginations, but as the sun set on that eventful day, her barely conscious and abused body lay on the tideline of the beach. From that day on she detested and feared the touch of water or any other liquid on her body, but more significantly she vowed that all men who plied their livelihood on the sea were now her mortal enemies and like rats or other vermin deserved no other fate than a slow lingering death, and what better way to promote this vow than by joining the ranks of the bold buccaneer brigade.

Sally took leave of her family and sailed off for a new life in the Americas. Over the next few months, Sally visited many of the seedier waterfront bars and brothels along the Eastern US seaboard, seeking and recruiting women who held similar views to hers regarding seafarers of the male sex. To purchase a vessel to enact their pirating activities, this wicked bunch plied the world's oldest profession, but with a difference. On payment after services not always rendered, the clients were first relieved of all their cash and belongings and then cruelly castrated. This painful inhuman act became the subject of the colours which were flown proudly from the ship's mainmast. Surprisingly the business did not last long when news of the parting act became universally known, but long enough for the ghastly girls to purchase their first vessel, which they renamed – 'Maneater'.

As they set sail on their maiden voyage, Sally took stock of the motley crew of depraved women and duly appointed the most wicked among them to the various seafaring posts. Ruthless Ruthie she made her first mate, Dirty Debbie was to be 2nd mate, Lascivious Lizzie was chosen to act as boson, Lusty Lucille was appointed ship's cook, Murderous Molly, Chesty Charity and Jiggly Jugs Jenny were selected as 1st, 2nd and 3rd officers respectively, while all the ladies from the back room of the 'Old Cock Inn' were assigned as deckhands.

It did not take long for horrific tales of the homicidal exploits of this all girl gang of brazen buccaneers to reach all the trading routes of the seven seas; these included news of the good ship 'Attica' which was ambushed, attacked and annihilated in the Atlantic, the brigantine 'Pauline' was pounced on and pulverised in the Pacific. Off the coast of Caracas, the combined crew of the 'Cockleshell' were captured and castrated with cutlasses, whilst in the middle of the Mediterranean the matelots and midshipmen of the massive schooner 'Midas' were subjected to murderous molestations, which left the majority murdered and the few survivors mightily mutilated.

This then was the wicked trade plied by these bedevilled buccaneering bitches and as the 'Maneater' closed in on 'Lionheart', Captain Beauregard Templeton knew that to engage these mangy and unwashed sea-cats in battle was useless; the only way he could possibly save himself and his crew was by somehow outwitting them.

Grappling irons were flung from the 'Maneater' and before you could say 'castration', the blood-crazed bitches were swarming across the deck of the 'Lionheart'. Despite Captain Templeton's intentions, the attackers were in no mood for negotiations and soon the decks were awash with blood, gore and other male appendages (one in particular had taken Beauregard's eye and despite the mayhem around him, he wished he had known this big sailor a little better).

It was all over very quickly and soon Captain Templeton was the last man standing. Sally walked slowly towards him with raised cutlass in hand and murder in her eye – The captain spoke.

"Spare me oh merciful Sally and I will make you the richest woman in the world." Now Sally may have been far from merciful but she was certainly not stupid. She reckoned that by now she had emasculated enough sailors to consider the debt to her honour paid and to retire as a rich woman was certainly an interesting proposition. She came up to his side and uttered the one word,

"How?" The captain then told her of the cargo they were carrying which was 2000 butts of fine Malmsey wine, except that one butt was filled to the brim with gold, diamonds and other precious jewels and only he knew which butt the treasure was in.

Sally thought carefully about this proposition. She realized that she and her crew only had to open each butt before eventually locating the one with the treasure – and yet two things bothered her. Searching through 2000 butts would take time and being greedy as well as evil, did she really want her crew of callous cut-throats to learn of the treasure, knowing then she would have no choice but to share it if they did?

The captain sensed what was going through Sally's mind and so suggested that she order her crew back to the 'Maneater' while she had sport with the luckless captain before relieving him of his own 'Crown Jewels'. The ploy appeared to be working and the blood-soaked women, somewhat reluctantly, made their way back to their quarters. Finally, the two were alone and Sally raised her cutlass menacingly and demanded to be led to the butt containing the treasure.

Captain Templeton guided her nervously to the stairway leading to the lower deck where the butts were stored. He made a rapid calculation and pointed to a butt. Sally's heart was racing as she hurried towards the butt that was destined to change her life for ever – It certainly was, but not quite in the way that she had anticipated.

She wrenched off the wooden lid but due to its height she could not see inside it. She ordered the captain to lift her up so that she could survey the treasure, which is just what he hoped she would do.

"I can still see nothing you idiot, lift me higher," which is exactly what the captain did. He lifted her so high in fact that she overbalanced and fell headfirst into a butt of – fine malmsey wine.

The sun had set and darkness had descended as Captain Templeton raced up the stairway, cast off the grappling hooks and under the cover of darkness the 'Lionheart' pulled slowly away from the 'Maneater' and in less than an hour the pirates' vessel was little more than a smudge on the horizon. He allowed himself a satisfactory smile. As far as he knew, he was the only man to have ever outwitted Sinister Sally and lived to tell the tale. As he retired to his bunk that night, he thought of the reward he would receive when he presented her pickled corpse to the naval authorities....

Captain Beauregard Templeton awoke briefly, before he was destined to meet his maker with a pain too horrible to contemplate in his groin area. Standing over him triumphantly was a wine-soaked Sally with a blood dripping cutlass in her right hand and a gory mess clutched in her left that modesty forbids me to describe in detail. With his eyes gradually dimming, the captain stammered what was to be his final dying word, "H-h-how?" Sally cackled wildly as she explained her escape to the fast-fading captain. It transpired that as well as being the cruellest pirate that ever lived, it was well known among her murderous companions that she could drink any man or woman under the table and that Malmsey wine just happened to be her tipple of choice.

When she found herself immersed in the butt she had immediately started drinking until the vessel was drained of its contents and she was saved from drowning. It had taken a little longer than expected as she had to climb out of the butt three times for a wee – And now she had wreaked her revenge on the luckless captain....

Deprived of a treasure that had never existed, Sally returned to her dastardly crew and for the next five years they continued to terrorise the oceans of the world until she eventually retired and returned to her roots in Barton Bottoms where she met and married the local vicar and where she bore and raised nine children before passing away peacefully in her 90th year....

And though three centuries have elapsed, local rumour has it that her spirit still roams the pubs and clubs of her home town in search of debauched and dissolute women to form another pirate crew. These rumour mongers also suggest that if this was so then in Barton Bottoms she would probably be spoilt for choice!

<u>Soldier Soldier Won't You Marry Me?</u>

Sarah Cook was a strikingly handsome young woman of 18 summers. Her long titian tresses spilled over a fulsome bosom, reaching almost to her slim waist and framing a perfectly symmetric face of rare beauty, flawless complexion and beguiling allure. It was therefore no surprise to learn that nearly every eligible youth and young man in the parish of Barton Bottoms sought to be her constant companion.

Her father, Samuel Cook, who was mine host at the Mermaid Inn that stood on the banks of the river that flowed through the village, was very much aware of her outstanding beauty and as her only parent, due to the untimely departure of her mother (she had run away with a tax collector some three years ago,) he was constantly fending off unwanted attention from would-be suitors.

However, despite her father's over protectiveness, not all the attention paid to her was in vain. There were two rather handsome lads in the village who were often rewarded with a sweet smile as she served them drinks from behind the bar of her father's inn. William Green and Adam Strong had been pals since their schooldays and you rarely saw one without the other they were that close. William, or Billy as he was known by all, worked in the local smithy run by his father, whilst Adam occupied his time behind the counter of his family's ironmonger's establishment. The pair of them, as well as being the best of friends, were very accomplished horsemen and spent most of their spare time racing each other across the village common.

It was after one of these gruelling encounters, whilst sitting on the bench outside the 'Mermaid', each enjoying a flagon of porter served by the fair hand of Sarah herself, when they were joined by an army recruiting sergeant who just happened to be in the area. It was now 1815 and the news was that Napoleon had escaped from exile in the hopes of restoring his position as Emperor of France. Despite his last setback on the battlefield, which had led to his exile on the island of Elba, 'Old Boney', once again, was intent on raising yet another army to harry the British troops and their allies to realize his ambitions.

The Duke of Wellington, the Commander-in-Chief of the army, was determined to put an end to the 'Little Corporal' once and for all. To this end, he had tasked his generals to gather together a great army by sending out recruiting teams to all corners of the British Isles and offering the 'King's Shilling' to any male who looked capable of shouldering a rifle, wielding a sabre or riding a horse.

It was this third ability that had caught the attention of recruiting sergeant Tom Steel.

"Here lads, let me pay for those," he offered, passing a florin over to Sarah, who accepted it with a little curtsey. "What's two fine fellows like you doing racing across an English meadow with no quarry in sight. Now wouldn't it suit ye both better to be doing the same with sabre in hand chasing them pesky 'Frenchies' and chopping a few heads off," he grinned, wiping the froth from his greying moustache. "The pair of you dressed in bright scarlet jackets and white pantaloons, what young lassie could resist such fine manly figures?" he added, making a sly glance at a now blushing Sarah.

Billy and Adam laughed at this suggestion but it was not without some merit. Both had set their caps at the delightful Sarah and both retained aspirations of their attentions not being unrequited. The drinks continued to flow and it was plain to see that sergeant Steel's persuasive manner was winning the two young men over. As the sun was setting on that momentous day it illuminated two rather shaky signatures on a very official looking document – recruitment papers for the 13th Hussars....

There was little doubt that both Adam and Billy appeared to have been born for military service and as Sergeant Steel had predicted, many of the ladies of Barton

Bottoms were in thrall of the dashing pair who paraded the village in their smart new uniforms and none more so than Sarah Cook, who's heart skipped a beat that night as they entered her father's inn – Yet that beat was just a little faster as Adam smiled and winked in her direction.

It was less than two weeks later when Adam and Billy received the news that their regiment would be setting sail for Europe in the next few days. During this period, Adam and Sarah were inseparable and so quickly and deeply did their devotion grow that much to her father's annoyance and Billy's jealous nature, the pair had become engaged and had sworn their undying love for each other with Sarah promising to be Adam's bride on his safe return...

The Battle of Waterloo proved to be a bloody affair with significant casualties on both sides. The 13th Hussars were in the thick of it from the start and the regiment charged repeatedly during the day and completely routed a square of French infantry. Both Adam and Billy played their parts heroically only for Billy to see his friend and comrade-in-arms unseated from his horse on the final charge and disappearing under the hooves of the enemy's battle-crazed horses. He was never to see him again that day and feared the worse....

News of the battle and subsequent victory for Wellington's forces reached Barton Bottoms a day or two later and Sarah was distraught to learn that Adam had been struck down in the fighting although his body had never been accounted for. She found some comfort in the safe return of Billy as he related to her the bravery of her man. He too was saddened at the loss of his best friend, yet his love for Sarah surpassed any feelings of guilt for his ungentlemanly conduct as within a month of the terrible news he had declared these feelings to Sarah by asking for her hand in marriage.

Sarah was taken aback at this bold proposal. She still harboured a belief that her beloved Adam would return one day, yet despite her grief and the promise made to him on his departure, she knew that hard times lay ahead and that without the protection of a man she would be vulnerable. She thought long and hard on Billy's proposal before she gave him her answer.

"Until Adam's death is confirmed or until three years have passed, I shall remain faithful to my vow. If by then he has not returned, then I shall marry you" ….

It was almost three years to the day when Sarah received the letter. It informed her that Adam, who had suffered such wounds that he had lost his memory, had been carried from the field and cared for by a Belgium farming family, was indeed alive and well and had regained his memory and was returning to make her his bride – Sarah was overjoyed – Billy was not!!!

A further month had passed and there was no sign of Adam's return. The month turned into a year and still he kept his distance. Billy did his best to persuade Sarah that whatever the reason, Adam was not returning and that they should marry – but his pleas were in vain. She had doubted his existence once and vowed never to do the same again. Each year, on the anniversary of the cursed letter being received, Billy renewed his petition to Sarah and each year he received the same negative response….

Thirty years had passed and Billy had long gone to meet his maker; a bachelor to his dying day. Sarah never gave up hope and each day she would stand on the bridge that spanned the river, scanning the road beyond for the return of her lover – It was to be in vain.

That year brought a great drought to the area and the river, for the first time in living memory, ran dry. The weir, which was just downstream from the bridge was fully exposed and it was then that the horrific discovery was made. Wedged under the bottom stones of the weir was a skeleton, the bones picked clean by the rushing waters and the fishes. Normally it would have been impossible to identify the bones except that on one of the skeletal fingers was a gold ring inscribed with the intertwining letters 'SC' and 'AS' – There was no doubting that this was indeed the remains of Adam Strong.

The inquest concluded that Adam was indeed returning home all those many years ago, and must have fallen from the bridge, had drowned and his body carried along the river to be caught under the lower stones of the weir. It would probably never have been discovered if it hadn't been for the drought.

However, if a more diligent examination of the skeleton by the coroner's office had been carried out, they would surely have queried the jagged furrow along the rib bone closest to the heart, probably caused by a sharp implement. However, covered by thirty years of silt, they would probably never have discovered the military style dagger bearing the barely distinguishable initials - 'WG'.

The Escort

Samantha Croft, or Sami as she was known to her friends, was bored. Some would say that she was an ungrateful bitch as she appeared to have everything that a woman could possess; Phillip, a loving, hard-working and handsome husband, three lovely kids, a house in Barton Bottoms to die for and a well-paid but challenging career. Despite all this she felt that there was little new or exciting in her life and at 35 she believed that time was not on her side. Although she did not realize it at the time, all this was about to change.

A new girl had recently come into the office and as fate would have it she was allocated a desk next to Sami's. Her name was Lucy and although she was much younger than Sami, she was reminded of herself at that age. It was not surprising therefore that there was an immediate rapport between the two of them and as well as sharing their lunch breaks they had got into the habit of visiting the local wine bar at the end of the working day and sharing a bottle of Pinot.

It was inevitable that sooner or later the conversation would turn to relationships. They were part way through the second bottle when Sami, emboldened by the wine, confessed her dissatisfaction with her current tedious lifestyle that had become boring beyond belief, with the same old rituals been observed week in and week out; she smiled ruefully when she admitted that the annual summer holiday would be spent in Bournemouth – for the tenth consecutive year.

"How are things in the bedroom department?" inquired Lucy with a wicked smile. Sami was a little taken aback at first with this rather personal question and her rapidly reddening cheeks reflected her discomfiture. "OK, I guess," she replied with her eyes downcast. "Let me hazard a guess," interjected Lucy. "Twice a week, on the bed, missionary position, ten minutes' max' and him snoring five minutes later." Sami's rosy cheeks took on a deeper hue yet she had to admit that Lucy's vivid and forthright description of her love life was not that far removed from the truth as she nodded in agreement. "It doesn't have to be so boring," Lucy suggested with a somewhat enigmatic smile. "I could show you how you can spice things up just a little, or even quite a lot, depending on your – let's say – requirements!"

To say that Sami was interested would be an understatement. The alcohol was certainly doing its work and yet all inhibitions had not quite deserted her – yet. "I'm not sure what you are suggesting Lucy," she replied, "But don't forget I'm a married woman with kids," she added.

"So am I," responded Lucy, "But it didn't stop me joining the agency." Sami's initial fascination had now morphed to intrigue and she begged Lucy to tell her more.

"It was about three years ago, and like you my life with Clive was becoming boring," Lucy began. "And then I came across the card pinned up in the local shop, *'Male and female escorts required – Good rates of pay – Contact Ray on 774*******5.* I rang the number, had an interview with Ray and 3 days later I took on my first job. It was with an old guy who was attending a formal dinner and needed some eye candy to accompany him. It was a fabulous night; he wined and dined me, paid me gracious compliments and behaved like a perfect gentleman all night. As I stepped into the taxi that he had ordered for me at the end of the night, he slipped a £50 note into my hand."

Sami listened in awe at what her new-found friend was telling her and found it difficult to believe it was that easy to have such a good time and get paid for the privilege. "So, there's no – no – er – hanky panky involved then?" asked Sami suspiciously.

"Well that all depends," replied her friend knowingly. "Encounters can be as innocent or as naughty as you want. Take the old guy; he was more than happy just to have me on his arm but my next job was a totally different proposition. Turned out he was a banker in the city and rolling in it. He introduced himself as Roger and was attending some prestigious banquet and being recently divorced he needed an escort for the evening. I expected to see another old dodderer but blow me when Roger turned up I thought it was Brad Pitt's brother; rich and handsome to boot – Oh, I forgot to add, randy as well. After the fourth glass of champagne I decided to stop knocking his hand from my knee while we dined, which was probably a mistake as where it ended up almost caused me to choke on my fillet mignon." Both girls laughed out loud at this latest confession but Sami was further intrigued at Lucy's bold revelation and urged her to continue with the tale.

"I was feeling a little woozy with all the champagne and decided a trip to the 'Ladies' was in order. As I was refreshing my lippy, who should walk in as bold as brass but Roger, my date for the night, holding what I thought in my drunken stupor was a bottle of champagne. Turned out to be something quite different but he was still eager to share it with me." Once again, the tale was interrupted as the girls giggled even louder than before. "I then discovered Roger had booked a room for the night and it would have been impolite to refuse his invitation. When I awoke the following morning, it was to discover that Roger had gone, but not before he had left a little note that said, 'one for each encounter' and to which he had pinned eight £50 notes."

Sami's eyes widened and her face displayed a look that was a little of surprise, a smidgen of awe but for the most part it was that green-eyed monster - jealousy. Without the drink, I'm confident that Sami would have said no more about this 'Brief Encounter' but as she drained the final glass she found herself saying, "Have you still got Ray's number....?"

It was no time for regrets or second thoughts. Despite having several doubts about the downside of joining the agency, thanks to the persuasive nature of her friend Lucy she had indeed done so. She had experienced several dummy runs to learn the secrets of successful escorting and although Ray insisted she was ready for the real thing she was not as confident. Despite having these fears, she now found herself walking into the smartest hotel in Barton Bottoms to meet her first customer.

All manner of thoughts ran through her tortured mind. What would he be like? Would he be old or young? Ugly or handsome? Randy or well-behaved? Would he be satisfied just to enjoy her company or would he be looking for extra benefits as the night wore on. These and many other feelings almost caused her to stop and retrace her steps and then she recalled how excited Lucy had been when relating her adventures and her resolve returned and she eventually convinced herself that all would be well.

She had no worries about arriving home late as Phil', her husband, was attending a lodge dinner that evening and had booked in at the local Holiday Inn for the night as he would be in no fit state to drive home.

As she was about to enter the hotel she ran through the crib sheet that Ray had prepared for her. Her man would be sitting on a bar stool in the lounge bar. He would be sipping a gin and tonic and wearing a white carnation in his lapel.

Her hand shook and her lips visibly trembled as she smiled guiltily at the uniformed doorman who gave her a knowing wink. Gosh, do I look that obvious she thought as she pulled on the hem of her mini skirt, wishing that it was perhaps an inch or two lower. Her low-cut blouse did little to disguise a still impressive Décolletage and it was obvious that the doorman had seen for what she was, not exactly a tart but not that far removed.

She passed through the revolving door at the front of the hotel and was greeted with a similar curl-lipped look from the imperious concierge. It was much too late now for second thoughts and recriminations, the die was well and truly cast and if nothing else she just had to bluff it out.

She entered the bar and scanned the many occupied stools in search of her man – but there was no sign. One thing did puzzle her however. What on earth was her husband Phil doing perched on a bar stool, sipping a large gin and tonic and wearing a white carnation in his lapel???

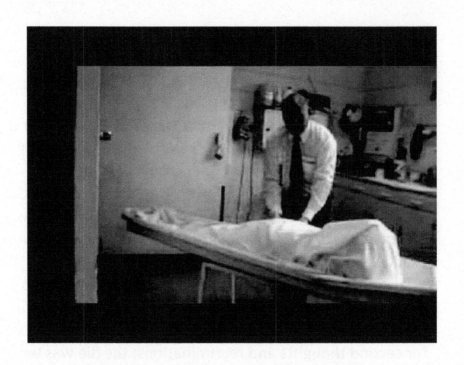

Death is the Final Joke!

Pete threw the letter across the room in utter disgust. For the past 15 years, he had been involved in the training and development of young athletes in Barton Bottoms and the surrounding area and now the local authority were informing him that due to recent government cutbacks, his position as assistant head coach for athletic development was to be made redundant.

"Gosh dad, what on earth's up with you?" exclaimed his daughter Melanie. "I've never seen you look so angry, not since that day mum gave your best trainers to the charity shop by mistake," she added with a wide grin. "You never did get them back, did you?"

"It's much worse than that my girl; they've only given me the chop from my coaching role. What am I supposed to do now for a job? Coaching young athletes is all I know and positions like that are not easy to come by, especially around here – and what's your mum gonna say with no money coming in. Her little job at the school certainly won't pay the bills or put food on the table. I'll have to send her out on the streets and she may bring in a pound or two," he added with a wry smile.

"Oh, dad you are awful, I've a good mind to tell her what you said," replied his daughter in mock anger. "But stop worrying, I'm sure we won't starve. I've got my job at the surgery, Jenny's due a promotion in her secretarial role in the front office of Barton Bottoms FC and I'm sure Charlie will chip in as well with her waitress money from Geppetto's. The other siblings nodded in agreement and Pet felt proud that he had brought up such considerate offspring's, although it must be said they were not always as selfless.

"I appreciate the offers girls but it's not just the money, I'm useless just sitting around doing nothing and I can imagine what your mum would think about that; no, I've just got to find a fresh job somehow."

Later that evening when Pete was thumbing through the 'situations vacant' section of the local paper, his daughter Melanie came bursting into the living room in a state of great excitement. She had been out with her boyfriend Joey and was obviously eager to impart her news. Pete was not in the best of moods due to the day's events and expected her revelations to be that she was either pregnant or about to elope (on reflection he thought that the latter may not be such a bad thing as the thought of having to fork out for three weddings

sometime in the near future scared the pants off him –
However, the thought soon faded).

"Dad, you won't believe this but you know that Joey
works at the hospital as a porter." Pete nodded his
agreement. "Well it so happens that one of his fellow
porters has left quite suddenly and the hospital trust are
desperate to replace him. Joey says he can put a good
word in for you if you are interested." Pete's initial
reaction was somewhat negative. Pushing a trolley around
all day with the sick and dying on board was not his idea
of a smart career move. However, the newspaper had
yielded nothing but equally lousy and dead-end jobs so on
balance the job as a hospital porter would at least keep
the wolf from the door until something better turned
up....

It was Pete's first shift in his new position and he found
himself teamed up with Joey, who was tasked in teaching
him the finer points of pushing a trolley around the vast
area of the hospital. Pete soon realized there was more to
this job than he had realized. There were 24 wards of
various sizes, 8 specialist clinics, the X-Ray and A & E
department and of course, deep in the basement - the
mortuary.

Joey was a nice enough lad at heart but over the years
had acquired the reputation of being a bit of a practical
joker. Pete smiled to himself when he remembered the
first time that Melanie had brought him home. He had
slipped a whoopee cushion under Sally's chair and he
would never forget the look on his wife's face as she sat
down. Joey never batted an eyelid but stared

unconcernedly up at the ceiling looking like innocence personified. These and many other stunts he had pulled over the past months on the Coker family but luckily for him they had taken it all in good part – well most of the time.

Over the next few days, Pete got into the swing of the job and was a little surprised to find that he was enjoying the experience, especially as there was never a dull moment with the young Joker about. The only occasion when the wide grin faded from Joey's face was when he had to deliver a cadaver to the mortuary. As he told Pete on a lunch break one day, the place gave him the 'willies'. He told him he frequently had nightmares of him entering the sombre room full of shroud-covered corpses, only to find one rising, the shroud slipping from a mutilated face and muttering something vague but without doubt, threatening.

Pete on the other hand had no such hang-ups and he felt compassion for Joey's obvious discomfort. He firmly believed that once you were dead that was it, unless your name happened to be Lazarus of course, but that was an entirely different ball-game. It was no surprise then when Pete offered to do all the runs to the mortuary so relieving Joey of what had been the journey he dreaded the most....

It was a late Saturday evening and Pete had volunteered to work Joey's shift as being a big supporter of Barton Bottoms FC he would have moved heaven and earth to attend the big derby game with local rivals, Loscock Hill Wanderers. Thanks to family connections with the club he had managed to obtain a ticket for the fixture that were proving to be as scarce as hen's teeth.

He heard the distant church clock strike midnight as he wheeled the shroud-covered corpse into the now empty mortuary. He had to admit that given the time and the place it was pretty scary and he could understand Joey's fear of the eerie place. He locked the trolley down ready for the mortician to prepare the corpse for a post mortem the following morning as apparently, it had been a somewhat suspicious and grisly death for the poor soul who lay motionless on the trolley.

Pete had turned and was halfway to the exit when he heard the noise. He glanced behind and was horror-struck to find the so-called corpse sat up. The shroud had slipped from the bloodstained face and Pete moaned in abject terror as his eyes were transfixed on the cruel-looking knife that was embedded up to the hilt in the dead man's skull. Slowly his initial panic subsided and as he approached the fearsome apparition, he realized who it was – It was Joey, who through lips distorted in pain croaked softly, "Look after her."

It was then the penny dropped. "You sly little bastard. You just can't help yourself can you. This is about the sickest joke you have ever pulled. Wait 'til Melanie hears about this and I think your courting days may be over." Joey nodded as though in agreement as he climbed down from the trolley and made his way to the sluice room. "Oh no you don't my lad, I want words with you," shouted Pete following what was proving to be a very lively corpse. He was less than a second behind Joey but when he entered the sluice room there was no sign of him. "Now how did he manage that the crafty beggar," whispered Pete as he searched in vain for the young prankster – but search as he did, it was in vain....

As Pete made his way home that morning he had to grudgingly admire the way that Joey had set up the elaborate hoax. The blood looked almost real, the face had a genuine death pallor and as for the knife buried deep in the skull, well that was truly a master stroke.

Pete parked the car in the drive and was surprised when Melanie came running from the house to greet him. "Oh dad, it's just terrible. There was crowd trouble at the big match yesterday with fights breaking out all over the terraces. It's just come on TV that there was one poor guy stabbed in the head but the police have not released his identity yet but apparently, he died from the wound. We'll probably get to know a little more about it when Joey comes to lunch later – Tears welled in Pete's eyes as he realized that this was highly unlikely!

Freud, He Aint

Young master Smith may have been named Sigmund but a Freud he certainly was not. His parents had great hopes for him in the twin fields of psychology and psychiatry with hopes that one day he would follow in their considerable footsteps and in due time might even graduate to psychoanalysis, a discipline in which they both excelled.

Frederick and Gretchen Smith were so skilled in this art that within an hour of sitting down with a person, they knew them better than they knew themselves – and they were seldom wrong in their analysis. Their successes in this field including spotting a man with suicidal tendencies before he became an airline pilot and alerting a hospital to a nurse who just loved experimenting with various poisons.

Despite attending the finest psychology academies in Europe, Sigmund barely scraped through the various examination stages and although he tried desperately hard to attain the standard that his parents expected of him, it appeared highly unlikely that this goal would ever be achieved.

Seeking meaningful employment after graduating with a 3rd class degree was never going to be easy and it was thanks to the pulling of a few strings by his parents that he managed to secure a junior position with a large supermarket chain in their HR department. His job was to vet applicants for the various occupations required in the running of a large organization and from day one it was obvious that this was going to be no easy ride.

After several somewhat disastrous appointments that included placing a man who was allergic to fish behind the fishmonger counter and recommending a recovering alcoholic to work on the wine and spirit section, his manager decided that enough was enough. Sigmund was devastated, knowing that his parents would probably disown him for such a rapid fall from grace and so pleaded fervently for one last chance.

Despite severe misgivings, his manager reluctantly agreed. Due to several requests, the store was to open a crèche for the children of both   employees and customers. An experienced manager and a number of nursery assistants were required and Sigmund's task was to search for suitable candidates for the positions. He had been advised to begin his search in the store as the manager believed that there were potential candidates among the many young mothers who shopped there.

Determined to make this a successful mission, Sigmund was up bright and early the following morning and positioned himself by the entrance doors. His plan was to select mothers with young children in hand with the intention of following them around the store, believing that he would be able to assess suitability by the way they coped with their children.

He had not long to wait before the first opportunity presented itself when a young woman came through the door accompanied by a rather sullen looking girl of about 3 or 4 who she placed in her trolley. They had reached the cereal aisle and the young mother reached for one of the healthier options on display.

"Don't want them," shrieked the child from the trolley, "Want them," she added, pointing to a sugar laden variety. The young woman however took little notice as she placed her original choice into the trolley – the child screamed.

"Now don't fret Monica and try to remain calm. We have a long way to go yet." They continued around the various aisles and eventually came to the biscuit section and mum made a healthy selection.

"Don't want them," shrieked the peevish child once more. "They taste like poo," she added at the top of her voice. The young woman was embarrassed but very calmly said, "Now Monica, please don't lose it; we're almost halfway round." The child went quiet – that is until they came to the sweet and chocolate section.

"Want them and them and them," squealed the little brat, pointing at virtually every confection on display - and then tears began to fall.

"Don't cry Monica, we'll be through the checkouts in a few minutes and then you can go home and have a nice nap."

The rest of the shopping expedition continued much in the same way and yet at each outburst the young woman continued to exert a calming influence on her charge with similar soothing statements. Sigmund's check list was almost full of 'ticks' and they were all in the appropriate boxes. He fervently believed that not only had he discovered a young woman who was obviously tailor made for the position of a nursery aide but her child management skills were such that she could probably operate successfully as the crèche manager; a position for which Sigmund was determined to recommend her.

If there were any lingering doubts in his mind they were instantly dismissed at the checkout. As the young woman opened her purse to pay for her goods, the peevish child grabbed at it, scattering numerous coins all over the supermarket floor.

"Oh Monica, that was really very naughty, but don't cry and upset yourself further. We'll soon be back in the car away from all the people who are shaking their heads and laughing at us. When we get home, I'll make a nice hot drink and a little nap after and all the world will seem right again."

"What a trooper," Sigmund muttered to himself, thinking how fortunate he was to have made such a rare discovery so early in his search, and of all the plaudits he would receive from a grateful management for his astuteness.

It was at this point that Sigmund introduced himself to the young woman and explained to her part of the reason he had been following her around the store. Before she had a chance to respond, he proceeded to tell her of a great career opportunity that the store was about to put to her. The young lady appeared most interested with Sigmund's rather enigmatic offer as she had been without permanent employment for some time.

"So just what is the job you are offering me? inquired the woman. "It sounds as though it could be quite a challenge," she added with a smile.
"Come to the main office tomorrow at 10-00am and the head of recruitment will explain everything to you and with your obvious talents I don't think you will be disappointed. The young woman looked somewhat surprised at this as she was not sure what talents she had displayed whilst shopping with the errant child...

Sigmund could hardly wait to inform his manager Mr Grimsdale of his amazing success at finding not only a most promising nursery attendant so early in the search, but probably a natural contender for the post of manager for the proposed crèche. He showed him the completed assessment chart with ticks in all the right boxes. He also told him of all the soothing and comforting little speeches that the young woman had made to the infant to reassure her and in an effort to keep her calm.

There was little doubt that Mr Grimsdale was quite impressed by the way that Sigmund had performed this particular duty and he mused that despite his earlier misgivings, perhaps there was hope for him yet in his chosen field – He was quite looking forward to meeting this extraordinary woman the following morning....

The young woman had turned up bright and early for the interview that she hoped would change her working life for ever; a life which to date had been nothing more than a series of dull and dead end jobs. What had Sigmund seen in her? Was it the way she carefully considered all the offers before making a choice? Ye! That was probably it she thought. I bet they are going to offer me an advisory position with regards to selective shopping. Could be a job as a store detective I suppose or perhaps they'll employ me as a secret shopper or maybe even – Her reverie was interrupted by a beaming Sigmund, indicating that the selection panel were ready to interview her.

Mr Grimsdale smiled and invited her to sit in the chair provided.

"The position we are about to offer you carries great responsibilities, which of course comes with a salary that reflects the importance of the role. Do you think madam that you have what it takes to take on such an arduous and responsible role?"

"Well I suppose I could answer that question better if I knew just what position you were offering me."

"Oh! I assumed that Sigmund had already informed you," replied a rather puzzled Mr Grimsdale. "It's the position of Manager of the new Nursery Crèche we will be opening instore shortly – Now how does that sound to you? Would you be interested?"

"I'd rather stick pins in my eyes thank you. I hate kids, especially that little brat I was looking after for my sister yesterday; she should have been strangled at birth the spoilt little madam."

"But-but, I don't understand," stammered a perplexed Mr Grimsdale. "Sigmund was most impressed with the way you dealt with the tantrums of young Monica yesterday."

I'm Monica you idiot, the little sh*t is called Pandora and it's in a box with the lid nailed down where she belongs!"

As Sigmund left the room he was already mentally composing his letter of resignation.

Do Elephants Sometimes Forget?

It had been a tough period in the relative short life of Danny Roberts. Studying to be a veterinarian was a long hard process of three years' classroom room training and then a further year in the field for hands-on experience before one was considered to be qualified. However, Danny believed it to be worth the effort as since that memorable day when he witnessed his dog Trixie giving birth to a fine litter of pups, he had always dreamed of becoming a vet.

Danny had learned much in those first three years of his studies but was now eagerly looking forward to performing some real practical outdoor work. He would have been quite happy if he had been assigned to some grotty farmer's field in Barton Bottoms where he had been born and raised, but could hardly believe his luck when he discovered that he had been assigned an overseas posting in Kenya.

The placement was all that he could possibly ever have dreamed of. The veterinarian clinic was situated way out in the bush about 100 miles east of Nairobi and during the first few months of his posting he had been able to observe and treat just about every creature that inhabited that part of the vast country.

Danny had assisted the chief veterinarian surgeon in several interesting procedures which included a hernia repair on a hippo, helped administer powerful pain-killing drugs to a rheumatic rhino, a giraffe with gastric problems and a lion with laryngitis. These and many other surgical and medical dealings with exotic animals convinced him that this was the area in which he would practice his profession when he was fully qualified.

If there had been any lingering doubts regarding this chosen path, they were quickly dispelled after that one amazing day when he was alone in the bush. He had been tracking a female cheetah that had been wounded by an over amorous mate to assess the damage inflicted. As this mission carried an element of danger he was carrying both a rifle and a drug pistol.

He followed the blood trail left by the stricken animal that eventually led him into a stand of whistling thorn trees and sure enough there was the big cat panting hard from its exertions. Danny immediately saw the claw marks across the hind quarters of the beast and realized that they were not life threatening. He decided that no stitches would be required to close the wound, just a generous application of antiseptic cream would do the trick.

Although the cheetah seemed docile enough, Danny was taking no chances and with unerring aim he shot a drug-laden dart into the animal's flank and within minutes was administering a generous swathe of antiseptic cream on to the wound.

He was just finishing the task when he was startled by a sound behind him. He turned quickly to find a young bull elephant, not much more than a calf, standing less than a couple of metres from him. He instinctively reached for his rifle only to realize that it was propped up against one of the thorn trees – with the elephant standing in between him and the weapon. He reached for the drug pistol hoping that the anaesthetic charged dart would be strong enough to subdue the apparently agitated pachyderm.

Danny was about to pull the trigger when the young bull elephant lifted a foreleg, pointing it in the vet's direction – He immediately saw the reason for the animal's distress. Danny got down on one knee, inspected the elephants foot, and found a large piece of wood deeply embedded in it. As carefully and as gently as he could, Danny worked the wood out with his knife, after which the elephant gingerly put down its foot.

The elephant turned to face its apprehensive saviour. Would it be grateful for his assistance as without doubt such a disablement in the huge creature would have prevented it feeding properly or to keep up with the rest of the herd, which Danny could now see in the middle distance, motionless as though they were waiting for the return of the young wanderer.

With a rather curious look on its face, the elephant stared at him for several tense moments. Danny stood frozen, thinking of nothing else but being trampled. His fears proved to be groundless as eventually the huge animal lifted its head, trumpeted loudly, turned and walked away to join its companions. Danny never forgot that elephant or the events of that fateful day. Even the cheetah, as it recovered its senses, licked his hand as though in thanks and recognition of his tender administrations...

All to soon Danny's time in Kenya came to a successful conclusion and it was a surprise to no one when he graduated with honours as a fully qualified vet. He had little trouble securing himself a position and was more than happy to be employed as a veterinarian assistant in a wildlife safari park.

It was there that he met fellow vet Lucy Hunter and within 12 months they had become engaged and later that same year they were married. There were the usual issues to sort out prior to the wedding but the easiest one to resolve was the honeymoon destination. Danny had talked so much about his fantastic 12 months in Kenya that despite all the exotic locations in the world that were available to the couple, there was really no contest as to their ultimate destination. Within days of the ceremony, the loved-up pair were in a jeep, heading for the very animal medical centre where Danny had honed his not inconsiderable veterinarian skills.

The pair were welcomed with open arms as it transpired that two of the regular vets had been taken ill and the remaining staff were experiencing great difficulty in meeting the current workload. Danny and Lucy were only too happy to step into the breach as they were never happier than when they were treating their beloved animals – and there was always the star-filled tropical nights for them to enjoy the fruits of marital bliss.

Fate is an unpredictable mistress as their first assignment took them to that same stand of whistling thorns where Danny had removed the huge splinter from the grateful animal's foot. Lucy remarked with a laugh that she wouldn't be surprised if the elephant was there to greet them, reminding her husband that elephants never forget – And would you believe it, as they entered the trees, who should be standing there but – No, it wasn't the elephant, but with the claw marks now faint but still visible along its flank, Danny knew instantly that it was the very cheetah that he had treated so many years ago.

It purred like a contented cat and came slowly towards them. Lucy, despite her training, slipped behind Danny wondering what would come next. Danny extended his left hand to the apparent docile creature while his right hovered over the drug pistol hanging loosely from his belt. There fears were unfounded. The cheetah, as it had done before, gently licked his outstretched hand as if in thanks for his kind ministrations in the past. Satisfied that she was among friends, the cheetah turned her head and growled softly. There was a rustle from the undergrowth as two small heads appeared, eyes blinking as they emerged into the strong midday sun.

Mum sat down proudly as the cubs approached the humans, knowing that a matronly all clear had been given. For the rest of that long yet unforgettable day, animals and humans delighted in each other's company. With the shadows gradually lengthening, the cubs scampered over to mum for their supper – and Danny and Lucy decided that it was time for them to go....

It was some 12 years later and with very successful careers behind them when Danny and Lucy were invited to the world-famous Beijing Zoo in China in order to take delivery of two panda cubs that were being donated to the zoological park where they were now employed.

On their way to the panda park they had to pass the elephant enclosure. Standing at the fence was a large African bull elephant. They stopped to admire the huge creature and were amazed as it lifted its leg several times whilst trumpeting loudly, all the while staring fixedly at Danny.

"I don't believe it," said Danny excitedly. "I think it's the same elephant that I helped all those years ago in Kenya." As if understanding his every word the creature nodded its head in agreement. Remembering the incident with the cheetah, Danny was determined to allow history to repeat itself.

Before anyone could stop him, Danny had scaled the high reinforced steel fence and dropped almost at the feet of his long-lost 'friend'. The elephant once again raised its leg, trumpeted even louder, wrapped its trunk around one of Danny's legs and slammed him hard against the railing, killing him instantly.

And the moral of this little homily is that while cheetahs seldom cheat, elephants sometimes forget!

Star Crossed Neighbours!

The Montgomery's and the Capstick's had not always been enemies. It had been some 20 years previous when the two newly wed couples had moved into the recently built estate on the outskirts of Barton Bottoms, Ronnie and Rosie Montgomery had moved into number 21 Verona Gardens and some 3 days later they were to meet their new neighbours Tim and Julie Capstick who had purchased the adjoining semi at number 23.

They shared so many common interests that they had hit it off immediately and as the years passed they became the firmest of friends. Each Saturday afternoon the two couples would catch the bus into the nearby town and while Rosie and Julie went shopping, Ronnie and Tim would make their way to the Barton Bottoms football ground to cheer on their local club. They would meet up later in the town centre for a meal and a few drinks and had often caught the last bus home together to their smart little semis in Verona Gardens.

It was no surprise when some 12 months after moving in that Rosie announced to Ronnie that he was going to be a father. As he dashed next door to announce the good news to his friends, he bumped into Tim who was hurrying towards number 21 to make a similar revelation to their friends. It was in June of the following year when Rosie gave birth to a son who they called Romany and within hours Julie was delivered of a beautiful daughter who they named Juliana.

The births had drawn the two families even closer and it was inevitable that their respective offspring's would also forge similar ties and they were seldom seen except in each other's company.

It was however a great surprise and source of bitter disappointment to both families when similar twin births some two years later produced progeny that could not stand the sight of each other. The Montgomery's had been blessed with another son who they called Merrill while the Capstick's were also delivered of a baby boy who they named Tyrone.

From the moment that the two boys could walk they were constantly at odds with each other and bloodied noses and blackened eyes were becoming the order of the day and despite the best efforts of both their families there seemed to be no ready solution to the groundless enmity. Ever the optimists, on their 9th birthdays, the fathers of the two boys enrolled them into the Barton Bottoms junior football academy, hoping that a sporting activity would give them a common bond from which at least a mutual respect could be forged if not an actual friendship.

Alas it did not work out quite as planned by the two families. However, both boys turned out to be most proficient at the beautiful game, Merrill as a formidable striker and Tyrone as a redoubtable defender. It also became quite apparent to the coaches that the pair would never be able to play in the same team due to their animosity towards each other.

As a consequence, Merrill signed semi-professional forms and joined his equally proficient older brother Romany in the ranks of Barton Bottoms FC, whilst Tyrone was snapped up by local rivals Loscock Hill Rovers.

Both teams had experienced very successful seasons yet had never met as they played in different leagues – All this was about to change. The two teams had progressed well in the local end of season cup competition and after two thrilling semi-finals against stronger opposition, now found themselves facing each other in the grand finale.

Ever the optimists, the Montgomery's and the Capstick's saw this confrontation as a golden opportunity for a coming together once more of the two families, whose previous good relations had become somewhat strained due to the animosity between their respective sons. Little did they know at that time that the healing process had already begun as Romany and Juliana had been meeting in secret for many months and were biding their time before making public what had been a rather furtive liaison.

The day of the cup final had arrived and both teams were pumped up in anticipation of a hard-fought encounter. The usual pre-match ceremony had concluded and members of both families were heartened to see Merrill and Tyrone shake hands – was this to be a turning point in their previous thorny relationship? – they were to find out in the final dramatic minutes of what had been a bad-tempered encounter.

The scores were locked at one goal each when Merrill received a glorious pass from his brother. He raced towards the Loscock goal with only Tyrone and the 'keeper to beat. He was on the edge of the penalty area, the goal gaped invitingly as he drew back his foot in anticipation of scoring the decisive goal that would secure the cup when a searing pain shot through his standing leg. Unable to halt his progress by fair means, Tyrone had resorted to the dark arts of the game and had aimed a vicious kick at his hated opponent which not only sent him clattering to the floor but also broke his leg in two places.

There was an audible gasp from the assembled spectators who had witnessed such a despicable act and it was no surprise when the ref' waved the red card under Tyrone's nose while poor Merrill was stretchered from the field in agony.

It was somewhat of an anti-climax when Romany scored the resulting penalty and there was a restrained hush around the ground when he later received the cup from the local mayor.

The celebrations that night was somewhat muted. This was a great shame as it had been the occasion on which Romany and Juliana had decided to tell the world of their romantic association. Despite some misgivings, they decided that despite the unfortunate happenings earlier in the day that they would announce their true feelings for each other.

The subdued atmosphere among the gathering in the Barton Bottoms FC social club suddenly lightened as Romany, now hand in hand with Juliana, made his announcement. The whole room greeted the news with hoots of approval and cheered the now smiling couple wildly – all that is except for one lonely figure who stood in the shadows at the back of the room – It was Tyrone.

As Romany concluded his announcement, Tyrone sprang from the shadows brandishing a wicked looking knife. He lunged at Romany, his eyes filled with fury and hatred with only one desire in his heart, to prevent a closer union between the two families. Tyrone was so determined to complete his wicked mission that he did not see the outstretched foot of cousin Ben Montgomery until too late. He fell to the floor and the knife flew from his hand to land harmlessly at the feet of the terrified couple.

Watching this frightening scene unfold was Father Lawrence who ministered to both families and had been growing increasingly concerned at the escalating tension between the Montgomery's and the Capstick's and was determined to put an end to it.

"This enmity between you must cease," announced the holy father. "And I say peace be to both your houses and to ensure this I shall provide for you a Turtle Dove to signify concord and love between you all. The Montgomery's shall build the coop to house it and the

Capstick's will be responsible for its upkeep. This way the old bond will be renewed, yet woe betide the family who fails to carry out their allotted task as they will then feel my wrath. I shall visit your households each month to ensure that all is well"

Strange as it seems, this unusual solution for restoring harmony appeared to be working – Well it was until Father Lawrence's third monthly check up. He had been in the habit of visiting early in the morning with his dog Prince, who on that fateful day had raced ahead of its master. As the good priest arrived at the door of the coop, he found Prince sitting there – with a very dead Turtle Dove in its mouth.

Father Lawrence was panic stricken. After all his preaching, it now appeared that he would be held responsible for the untimely death of the bird and he feared that as a result the dwindling church congregations would decline to the point where he would lose his job. That thought alone prompted him to perform the rather un-Christian act that followed.

Ensuring that there was no one around to witness his dastardly act, he cleaned up the bird as best he could. He then balanced it carefully on its perch, hoping that whoever arrived first would assume it had died of natural causes. Satisfied with his work, Father Lawrence and his naughty dog returned home...

It was later that day when the priest answered the urgent ringing of the 'phone – It was Romero.
"Would you believe it Father, the poor bird died last night and we buried it with all due pomp and great solemnity.

But guess what? Some sad b*****d came and dug it up and placed it back on its perch – Can you believe how any human being could be so insensitive. I swear if I ever find the culprits I'll swing for them….

It was less than a week later that the parishioners of St Veronica's were amazed to discover that Father Lawrence had asked, nay demanded of the Bishop to be sent on permanent missionary work in the upper reaches of the Amazon!

A HALLOWEEN SURPRISE

Phil Cook was a marital cheat; or at least that was the considered opinion of his wife Sonia. All the usual signs were there, late nights at the office to work on so-called vital projects, conferences that took him away for days at a time, furtive telephone calls at all hours which nearly always resulted in him having to go out to resolve some problem or other, but the real clincher was the endless flowers and other small gifts he brought home at increasingly regular intervals, a sure indication of a man attempting to salve a guilty conscience with a stream of meaningless knick-knacks.

In truth, Phil was a high-flying executive in the nearby city and was never happier than when each stressful day came to an end, allowing him to return home to his large detached residence in Barton Bottoms and there to relax with a martini, a nice home-cooked meal and his devoted wife of nearly 7 years, who he loved dearly.

Despite his apparent devotion, Sonia was convinced that it was all an elaborate act to lull her into a false sense of security while he regularly engaged in extra-marital relations with his bit on the side or maybe he was frolicking with a succession of unsuspecting females – either way she was determined to find him out for the cheat that she convinced herself he was.

As each day passed, the thought of her Phil being a secret philanderer ate away at her like a worm burying deeper into a rotten apple. There was only one thing for it to preserve her sanity, she had to find out who was the trollop that was stealing her man – and god help her when she did find out.

The opportunity for Sonia to engage in her Miss Marple mission was not long in presenting itself. It was 9-00 o' clock the following night when Phil's mobile rung. As usual he made his usual feeble excuse and took the call in the kitchen. Ten minutes later, looking very shame-faced he returned to the lounge and informed Sonia that an emergency board meeting had been called and his presence was required.

Board meeting my eye, thought a most suspicious Sonia, more likely a 'broad' meeting in the empty offices of his company headquarters. But my lad, you aint getting away with it this time she mused as she made up her mind to follow him….

The office block appeared to be deserted as she shadowed him at a discreet distance to the board room. Without a pause, Phil entered the room, closing the door silently behind him. Sonia tiptoed over and placed her ear to the door. At first there was nothing to hear, and then –

a giggle that was undoubtedly feminine – Sonia burst through the door to find – about a dozen business executives looking most surprised at this sudden and unannounced intrusion to their high-powered meeting; the giggle coming from a middle-aged tea lady who had inadvertently dropped a cheese and pickle sandwich. Sonia made a somewhat pathetic excuse and quickly departed before Phil had time to see her.

Now you would be forgiven for thinking that after such a disastrous episode, Sonia would have learnt a very salutary lesson – but no! She was made of sterner stuff and if anything, it had made her more determined than ever to catch her husband at it; all she needed to do was wait patiently for the next opportunity – and it presented itself quicker than she had expected.

Always on the lookout for clues to her husband's supposed infidelity it was just a couple of days later that she stumbled across the ruby necklace. When I say 'stumbled', it was actually in his locked writing desk to which she had acquired a spare key many years ago.

Could it be for her she wondered? He had, like the dutiful husband he was, been showering her with little gifts for some time now but nothing quite as expensive as this obviously was. Then she remembered; they would be celebrating their 7th wedding anniversary soon and this was probably going to be her present – and if not then it would probably be adorning the neck of one of his 'floozies'. All she had to do was wait for the day and woe betide him if that ruby necklace was not among the anniversary gifts.

The day of their anniversary dawned and she wasted no time in opening the little assortment of presents that awaited her from family members and in particular, the one that she would receive from her husband. As copper is considered to be the material of choice for the 7th anniversary of marriage, she had bought him a copper hip flask and assuming that Phil knew nothing of these little rituals, she was more than happy to think that he considered a ruby necklace a suitable gift for their big day – or did he?

She was somewhat concerned when there appeared to be no gift from him among the little pile that she had now opened. She was even more surprised when he told her to close her eyes while he led her into the kitchen. On the command to open them, can you imagine the sight that met her eyes – a full set of copper-bottomed pans – the first thought that entered her enraged mind was, 'So which cheap tart is wearing my ruby necklace?' – she had not long to wait before the recipient was revealed….

As it happened, Phil's parents were soon to be celebrating their own wedding anniversary and Sonia had decided that with the room full of family friends, this would present the perfect opportunity to expose him for the cad that he was.

The function room of Barton Bottoms FC had been booked for the auspicious occasion and Sonia was revelling in the thoughts of the big disclosure she was about to make to the assembled guests. She walked onto the stage, turned on the microphone and was about to make her revelation when Phil's parents made their entrance. His mother looked a picture, wearing a most fetching dress, her hair beautifully coiffured – and around her neck the most beautiful ruby necklace that Sonia had last seen nestling in her husband's writing desk just a few days earlier – the penny dropped!

The necklace had never been intended for her or a shameless mistress but for his mother. Although somewhat rattled Sonia did not lose her composure as she announced over the microphone,

"Fellow guests, please join with me in greeting the happy couple on this their 40th anniversary – their Ruby Wedding!!!"

The resolving of the necklace issue did little to lessen Sonia's belief that her husband was 'playing away' and she was determined to catch him out with his infidelity – and the wherewithal presented itself the very next morning.

The local golf club were holding their annual Halloween Ball and had decided that this year it was to be a costumed affair. Sonia took no time in ordering two costumes; one of Batman for Phil and one depicting Wonder Woman for her, which she deliberately hid from her husband, telling him it was to be a surprise on the night.

On the appointed evening, Sonia came down with one of her migraines and told Phil that she couldn't possibly attend the ball in such a state but insisted that he should go and enjoy himself. He told her that this would be impossible without her presence but she was insistent and so very reluctantly he picked up his costume and off he went.

Sonia gave it an hour or so before gathering up her costume and followed him to the golf club. On arrival, she changed into her costume, confident that Phil would not recognise her but she certainly knew exactly who he was – besides being a serial cheat.

She soon spotted Phil cavorting around on the dance floor, dancing with every female he could, getting a little kiss here and a warm squeeze there. Sonia spied her chance and ensuring her mask was in place, approached him seductively. One glance at her outfit and he quickly ditched his current partner and devoted his time to this new babe who had just arrived. She let him do whatever he wished, feeling no guilt as after all he was her husband.

Finally, he whispered a little proposition in her ear and she agreed, so off they went to one of the cars and as they say, the rest was history. Just before unmasking at midnight, Sonia slipped away and went home, put the costume away and got into bed, wondering what kind of explanation he would have for his outrageous behaviour.

Sonia was sitting up reading when Phil came in. She asked how the evening had been? He replied glumly, "Oh, the same old thing darling. You know, I never have a good time when you're not there." Then she asked, "Did you dance much?" He replied,
"You know, I didn't dance even one dance. When I got there, I met Pete, Bill Brown and some other guys, so we went into the back room and played poker all evening. But I'll tell you something from what I heard, old Freddy had the time of his life.”
“Who on earth is old Freddy?” queried Sonia.
“He's the chap I lent my costume too!”

Lady Luck and Jim

Jim Rowbottom had, for many years now, considered himself to be one of the unluckiest guys on the planet. It had all started at St Audrey's primary school in the little northern town of Barton Bottoms where it was considered de rigueur that by year 4, all pupils where to be known to each other by their nicknames rather than the given name so lovingly chosen by their parents. The pupils were apparently well versed in creating meaningful nicknames for their fellows, derived from either their appearance, where they lived or in Jim's case their surname – and Paddle Arse was to haunt him for the rest of his schooldays.

Jim had always blamed this unfortunate event for the bad luck and misfortunes that dogged his heels for years to come and if Lady Luck truly existed then she was certainly no friend of Jim's. There was the time while still at school when the captain of Barton Bottoms FC, Jim Lord visited his class and gave cup final tickets to all the boys called Jim. Unfortunately, our Jim was at the local A

& E at the time getting stiches in his chin after tripping over a black cat and falling into the local window cleaner's ladder which fell onto his new bike leaving it with a twisted frame and two buckled wheels – are you beginning to get the picture.

His luck with the opposite sex was just as unfortunate and it had all stemmed from that first cinema date with Karen Brandiforth. She had forgiven him when he had tripped whilst returning with ice creams at the interval that were subsequently deposited in her lap. She had even excused his clumsiness when he had dropped her new handbag in a puddle whilst she put on her coat. However, even the saintly Karen could not forgive what happened as they were boarding the last bus home.

As they climbed the stairs to the upper deck, Jim once more missed his footing and instinctively reached out to grab something that would prevent him falling. It was unfortunate that the 'something' turned out to be the hem of Karen's skirt. It certainly cushioned his fall but as the skirt started its descent, to eventually finish up around her ankles, it revealed that for whatever reason she had decided that night to go 'commando'. At this revelation, a rather short-sighted old man seated opposite turned to his companion and said,
"I didn't think it was a full moon tonight Harry!" The response that Jim received from Karen on his request for a further date is unprintable.

The series of unfortunate events were not always of his own making. His first job after being asked to leave school early (he swore that the carelessly discarded cigarette butt that burned down the cycle shed was out) was as an office boy in a large multi-national corporation. The first couple of months passed incident free until that fateful day he had crossed the path of the company's CEO. The perplexed looking executive was standing in front of a shredder with a piece of paper in his hand. As Jim attempted to pass him the CEO grabbed his arm and spoke anxiously.

"Hey son," said the CEO, "This is a very sensitive and important document here, and my secretary has gone home ill. Can you make this blasted thing work for me?"

"Certainly sir," said Jim enthusiastically. He turned the machine on, inserted the paper, and pressed the start button.

"Excellent, excellent!" said the CEO, as his paper disappeared inside the machine. "This document will probably result in either the company making millions or going bust - I just need the one copy!" – Jim picked up his P45 the following day.

Life continued to throw a series of curve balls at Jim and he decided that a change of scenery might just possibly change his run of bad luck, and what better place to visit in order to test this theory than Las Vegas.

He had no success with the roulette wheel, the blackjack cards had been a nightmare and as for the craps table, well that was an interlude best forgotten. With a sigh of resignation, he was about to leave the casino when passing by the slots he noticed a gaming chip on the floor. He picked it up and as a last futile attempt to change his luck he fed it in to the nearest machine. The reels spun randomly and Jim was about to walk away when he was stopped dead in his tracks as the machine spewed out a succession of chips that mounted up to almost $500.

In that instant, Jim convinced himself that a lifetime of bad luck was now behind him and although the win was pretty substantial he convinced himself that this was just the start of a winning streak and that the machine in front of him was to be the catalyst of his good fortune.

For the next hour or so, Jim fed the insatiable machine with the $5 gaming chips until he realized that there was only one remaining. His fingers trembled as he reached towards the slot and it was no surprise when it fell from his hand and as though cursed it rolled across the room as though powered by an unseen force. Jim Jumped from the stool and chased after it. As he bent down to retrieve the chip he was startled to hear the blaring of assorted whistles and bells, the flashing of a kaleidoscope of brightly coloured lights and the clapping and cheering of other casino patrons, applauding the guy who had just won $1,000,000 from the very machine that Jim had been playing. Jim considered confronting the newly made millionaire but with a sigh of resignation realized that this would be fruitless as it was just another example of Lady Luck laughing in his face and kicking him when he was down.

And so, Jim continued with his life of unfortunate events and as a hobby he took to reading about rare and valuable antiques and the people who had made fortunes from happy chance discoveries. Of course, he was convinced that such a discovery could never possibly happen to him – or could it?

Jim was walking through the high street in Barton Bottoms one day when he noticed a mangy old cat lapping milk from a dish in the doorway of a store. The dish looked sort of familiar and with a gasp Jim realizes that he had seen a picture of that very same dish in one of his antique books and recalled that it had a minimum six-figure valuation. Jim walked casually into the store and offered to buy the cat for £2. The storeowner shook his head and replied,

"I'm sorry, but the cat isn't for sale." Jim was not to be put off so easily. "Please reconsider sir, I need a cat around my house as it's overrun with mice. Tell you what, I'll give you £20 for the cat." But the owner still refused. Jim was now doubly determined to get his hands on the dish and made a ridiculous offer of £100 for the cat. The owner scratches his head as though deep in thought before grudgingly accepting Jim's overpriced offer. Jim realized that he was almost within grasping distance from the dish and casually asked if the owner could throw in that old dish, adding that the cat was used to it and that it would save him from having to buy another dish. The owner sighed once more before replying,

"Sorry mister, but that's my lucky dish."

"How can a dish be lucky?" queried Jim, now quite exasperated.

"Well," replied the storeowner with a wicked grin, "I guess it's lucky because so far this week I've sold 68 cats."

As Jim left the store with the old cat tucked under his arm he was convinced that the sly chuckle he heard from above was from his old nemesis – Lady Luck....

You would have thought that after such a chastening experience, Jim would have learned his lesson, but as they say, there's no fool like an old fool. It was about a month later when passing the same shop that Jim spied a hand-written notice pinned to the door that read:

'SINGLE FEMALE with no baggage or previous encounters seeks male companionship. Looks, ethnicity and religious beliefs unimportant. I'm a young and very good-looking girl who just LOVES to play. I love long walks in the woods, riding in your car, hunting, camping and fishing trips, cosy winter nights lying by the fire. Candlelight dinners will have me eating out of your hand. Rub me the right way and watch me respond. I'll be at the front door when you get home from work, wearing only what nature gave me. Kiss me and I'm yours for £2,000 – Sounds expensive but remember, all the above are available at all times, day or night, and I'm yours for life. Call in the shop and ask for Daisy.'

Well I ask you, what single red-blooded male could resist such an offer. Jim had been a bachelor for far too long and perhaps the love and companionship of a good woman would certainly add some meaning to his life if nothing else. Jim entered the shop with his cheque book in hand and asked the shopkeeper to introduce him to Daisy. The shopkeeper looked Jim up and down rather disapprovingly and insisted on payment first. With some misgivings and not a little reluctance, Jim handed over a cheque and waited rather impatiently as the shop owner went into the back room of his premises. It was less than two minutes later that he returned leading the cutest 8-week old black Labrador retriever that Jim had ever seen...

It was at this moment in his life when events were destined to change for ever. It turned out that Daisy was the offspring of a former supreme champion at Cruft's. The two became inseparable and when Daisy's pedigree was proven and she was introduced to another former champion, the resulting pups were selling at four-figure prices.

As for Lady Luck? Well she's now a permanent resident in the Rowbottom household and all the past unfortunate events are now nothing but distant memories.

Cindy Goes Too Hollywood

Cindy had only ever harboured one ambition in her short but eventful life and that was to be a famous actor. To tread the boards or appear on TV would have been acceptable but her real all-consuming dream was to appear on the silver screen. She knew that the likelihood of her ever realizing her dream was slim but she was a born optimist and was ever hopeful that an acting opportunity would arise.

She was never happier than when sharing the sofa with other family members, watching a vintage musical or some other Hollywood blockbuster. However, there was little doubt that the feature length Disney animations were her favourites.

She would sit silently and totally enthralled through endless showings of 'Bambi'; She had seen 'Dumbo' so many times that the DVD was almost worn away, but there was no doubt that her all-time favourite just had to be 'The Lady and the Tramp'. The scene that always got her was when the 'Tramp' pushed the last meatball to his 'Lady'. It brought a lump to her throat every time.

Her break came sooner than she could ever have expected. She was enjoying a walk with the family one sunny afternoon down by the local river, when they came across a film crew, who appeared to be shooting scenes for a movie of some kind. However, it seemed that the cameras were not rolling as the family approached and all they heard were loud and angry voices.

"Where the hell has she got to?" shouted a chubby little man who appeared to be in charge. "She's such a spoilt brat running off like that; I don't know what on earth gets into her and just when we are about to shoot her big scene. Looks like another good filming day wasted and what's more......"

The chubby little man, who apparently was directing operations, stopped in mid-sentence, just as Cindy and the family came into his eyeline.

"I don't believe it," he muttered, casting his practised eye over the family. "Hey, Tony, see what I see?" he said to the younger guy at his side. "She's a dead ringer for Bess, same hair colouring and everything. I reckon we could use her in this final scene providing we get her guardian's approval that is.

The younger guy nodded his head in agreement and went over to the little gathering and singled out Geoff as being possibly the head of the family. He engaged him in earnest conversation and within minutes there was a nodding of heads and shaking of hands before Geoff told Cindy to follow the man to the riverbank. It was to be a non-speaking part and all that was expected of Cindy in her first film role was to sit quietly on the grass and run over to the man standing by the bridge when he called her name.

It was all over in one take. It was obvious that Cindy, even at such tender years, was a natural and the camera certainly loved her golden hair and big brown eyes that were destined to melt hearts for years to come. It turned out that there was to be a sequel to the film in which Cindy had played a bit part and the chubby little man who had first spotted her potential and fed up with the ever-growing tantrums of that diva Bess, had insisted that the role be offered to the up and coming young lady that he had discovered that day down by the riverside.

It was a good meaty part but not the lead, a position which everyone knew she would naturally be comfortable with and was something that would figure significantly throughout her life. Cindy was to play the part of a runaway, who after months of abuse and beatings and despite her tender years had decided to flee the family home and seek solace elsewhere.

There was no doubt that it was a role that she could really get her teeth into. In the storyline, Cindy travelled the length and breadth of the country seeking a better life and yet the fates appeared to continually conspire against her, until that fateful stormy night when she had sought shelter in a barn. She had been exhausted and was still dead to the world the following morning when a kind and caring farmer stood over her prostrate form and took pity on her.

Despite diligent enquiries, her family could not be traced and the farmer and his equally kindly wife took her in and made her a part of the family. As the years passed there was little doubt that she had turned into a real beauty and it was all the farmer and his wife could do to keep the amorous admirers away from their door. She had entered a number of contests where beauty, manners and elegance had been prerequisites and it was not long before trophies and certificates filled every room of the little farm and life appeared to be good. It was unfortunate therefore when she was run down by a tractor being carelessly driven by a neighbouring farmer while she had been out hunting with the man who had so kindly taken her into his home....

The film had been a rip-roaring success all over the cinema-going world and it was no surprise when Cindy was nominated to receive an Oscar for her poignant portrayal of the ill-fated heroine and offers for her to star in a succession of films was not entirely unsuspected. Each day Geoff, who had become her agent, would trawl through the many offers from film moguls worldwide.

They all appeared tempting, with 6-figure cash sums being offered for Cindy's services. However, the offer that thrilled the family most was the one that arrived with the Hollywood postmark and when opened turned out to be from none other than the world-famous director Stefan Burgspeils. He had envisaged a blockbuster along the lines of 'Planet of the Apes' but with one major difference. It was not just the apes who would be the dominant animals on Earth but would also include many other species in a sort of caste system but with humans being considered the bottom rung of the new social ladder.

Cindy was to be cast as the unassuming heroine who would fight tirelessly for the abolition of the system and where all living creatures would inhabit the Earth as equals. It was to be a mammoth project and a casting nightmare for Stefan and his team. Cindy however, was a natural. She had her role off to a 'tee' in no time at all while the animal trainers were having a torrid time in getting other cast members into shape. The tigers were tiresome, wanting nothing more than to eat their fellow thespians; the bats and owls insisted on night shooting only; the kangaroos wouldn't sit still for love nor money and as for the sloths, well, all they wanted was to hang around the studio and sleep all day.

However, Stefan had not become one of the greatest movie directors in the business through lack of initiative and more than once in his career he had turned what appeared to be unsurmountable adversity into resounding success. He decided to shoot a stunning trailer of the forthcoming film, using his leading man, Bid Prat, who was to play the starring role as the leader of a pitiful band of humans, determined to regain their rightful place in the pecking order and Cindy was to be his companion in this stunning drama.

It was a masterstroke. The trailer was adjudged to have been the finest ever made in Hollywood and though Bid played a most convincing role, it was Cindy that once again stole the show – This did not sit very well with Mr Prat as he believed his male ego had been well and truly pricked, having to play second fiddle to one who had made but a handful of movies while he had been a matinee idol for more years than he cared to remember – and he was determined to take his revenge on this jumped up little minx....

Filming had started in earnest. All the humans were at the top of their game and even the animals had finally got to grips with what was expected of them. However, it transpired that whenever Bid and Cindy were on the set together, he did everything in his power to belittle her; often complaining to Stefan that she was not the performer she was cracked up to be.

This went on for some time before Cindy decided enough was enough and she did what any self-respecting lady would do – In the middle of the final scene, she walked over to where Bid stood, complaining as usual – and peed all over his expensive crocodile shoes.

Bid recoiled in horror before declaring loudly that he would never work with dogs again. As for Cindy, she gave a triumphant bark, wagged her tail and trotted off like any self-respecting golden retriever would!

Murder at the Palace

The uniformed officer, licked the point of his pencil, cocked his ever-suspicious eye and harrumphed loudly before eventually turning to me with a look of total scepticism on his face and enquired.

"And you say you actually witnessed the fateful blow being delivered by the perpetrator that dispatched the innocent victim?" I felt more like the aggressor rather than just a witness under the baleful stare of the official before replying.

"Much to my horror officer, I did, and also the incident that led up to the brutal and unprovoked attack."

The week had started off so well. The wife and I had arrived at the popular seaside resort of Weston-Super-Mare under leaden evening skies but had awoken the following morning with the warm rays of the midsummer sun streaming through the rather flimsy curtains of our prettily situated seafront hotel.

After a most satisfying breakfast, we set off to explore the town and what delights it had to offer. The wife and I, over many years of holiday travels, had visited almost every corner of our fascinating land, yet for some unknown reason WSM had never figured high on our 'places to visit' agenda. It had always been the call of the Cornish and Devonian resorts that had attracted us in the past, giving little consideration of what the county of Somerset had to offer - So this was the year we were about to put that oversight right.

A pleasant stroll along the wide and expansive prom' brought us to the Grand Pier. We were tempted to explore it but decided to leave that experience for another day and so we crossed the busy road into the bustling town centre and were pleasantly surprised by the size and scale of the buildings, particularly the many retail outlets; well the wife was as I do believe she was born with a shopping bag in each hand. If retail therapy was an Olympic sport she would have accumulated a cupboardful of medals by now.

It had been our intention, as well as sampling the delights of WSM, to visit other places of interest within a reasonable striking distance of the resort. We had also planned to leave the car parked up and use the local bus services for our sightseeing. Well what's the point of reaching the age where bus travel is free and not taking advantage of it.

As 'She who must Shop' continued to search for those elusive bargains, I visited the local bus station to see what was on offer. I quickly realized that Bristol, Bath, Burnham-on-Sea and Wells were in reasonable striking distance and after a brief consultation with 'the boss', we mapped out our itinerary for the week. Little did we realize at the time that one of these destinations would prove to be the place where I was to witness the brutal and bloody slaying of two innocents.

Our first journey took us to the bustling city of Bristol and what a fascinating city it turned out to be. It is a port city known as the 'Birthplace of America'. John Cabot sailed from Bristol to help 'discover' North America in 1497 and for many years the city has played an important role in England's maritime trade in such goods as tobacco, wine, cotton and unfortunately was also heavily involved in the slave trade. It has many famous sons and daughters including artists 'Banksie' and Damien Hurst, J K Rowling, the creator of Harry Potter, actors such as Dave Prowse who played Darth Vader in the Star Wars series, John Cleese of Fawlty Towers fame and Hollywood legend Cary Grant (Archibald Leach), who were all born in or around the fascinating city of Bristol.

The wife got quite excited about Cabot, not unfortunately from an historic point of view but rather in the huge multi-story shopping mall, Cabot Circus, that had been named after the great sea-farer – she couldn't get enough of him, or rather the mall that bore his name.

I eventually persuaded her to leave this shopper's paradise with a promise that we would return (hopefully not in this decade) and as we were bussed home to WSM we planned our next trip which was to be to the smallest city in England – Wells. It was to be in this picturesque medieval city where I was to be witness to a dastardly crime – the brutal murder of two innocents.

On arrival at Wells, we left the bus station and strolled up the busy high street towards the cathedral quarter where we stopped for a bite to eat. I had set my sights on visiting both the cathedral and the Bishop's Palace gardens for a taste of culture, whilst the wife was once again in the mood for further exploration of the high street in the never-ending search for retail bargains...

We went our separate ways; she in search for a shopping mall while I passed through an ancient archway that led to the Bishop's Palace and decided on a stroll along the path adjacent to the moat that encircled this stately building – It was here that the deathly fracas began....

The officer harrumphed loudly once more and requested that I continue with my account of the murder. "This gang came swanning along as though they owned the place," I began. As I gathered my thoughts before continuing, the sights and sounds of this horrible tragedy came flooding back. There had been nine of them. The two obvious leaders of the mob where dressed all in white while their seven acolytes were more soberly attired in a shade of grey that did not flatter them.

They were cruising along, obviously disdainful of all others who shared their space when the two victims came into their vicinity in all innocence. I think it was curiosity on behalf of the female victim as she came too close to an equally inquisitive grey-clad gang adherent. The reaction from the larger of the white dressed gang member to this intrusion was instantaneous and brutal. He flew at the perceived intruder and with one mighty blow laid her lifeless, blood pouring from her mouth as she shrieked uncontrollably in her death throes. The remainder of the heartless and unfeeling band circled the twitching corpse as though this was just another everyday occurrence in their lives, with pity or empathy for the victim being in very short supply.

I suppose it was a natural reaction to the gruesome sight he had just witnessed for her male companion to dash to her side in the vain hope that she could yet be saved – It was probably not the wisest decision he could have made under the circumstances. The second of the white attired ones perceived this as a retaliatory move and before the brave but foolish male had got within a yard of his erstwhile companion, he was felled by a crushing blow, even more terrible than the first one delivered on his companion. It was surely enough to have rendered him equally lifeless and yet the maddened aggressor continued to rain blow after blow on the now unrecognisable form.

When the two gang leaders perceived that the intruders carried no further threat, they and their grey-suited entourage removed themselves quietly and coolly from the scene.

During the melee, there was one brief moment when I'd considered wading in to help the poor unfortunates, but quickly realized I would be in unfamiliar territory and was just as likely to be attacked as the hapless victims; and of course, there was the wife to consider. If I was not at our agreed meeting place at the prearranged time, what on earth would she do, apart that is from hoping that the life insurance policy was up to date – and so like many others before me, faced with a similar dilemma, cowardly discretion prevailed and I chickened out of a confrontation.

I of course relayed all these sickening observations to the officer who appeared to be taking it all very much in his stride, as though this type of event was an everyday occurrence in the Bishop's Palace gardens.

"Did anyone else witness the attack?" queried the officer. I told him that there were others around at the time but like me they appeared extremely distressed but utterly helpless. He again shook his head before remarking stoically, "Aye, that's the usual reaction from tourists. Us locals are quite used to such goings on as we get two or three similar incidents every year. It's the way of things in these parts.

To say I was shocked would be an understatement. Here was a man employed as a protector of those not always able to protect themselves and yet treating such deaths as mere everyday happenings. Unable to control my feelings, I blurted out,
"And is there nothing that can be done?"

The uniformed RSPCA officer shook his head before ruefully replying that ducks never seem to learn their lesson. They should never swim too close to swans, especially when there are cygnets about!

The End

(Until the next edition)

Lightning Source UK Ltd.
Milton Keynes UK
UKOW01f1226230817
307784UK00002B/140/P

9 781786 979438